And the Angels Sang

Lorina Stephens

Published by Five Rivers
www.5rivers.org

And the Angels Sang. Copyright © 2008 by Lorina Stephens

Cover art, *The Watcher*, original oil, by Kelly Stephens: Copyright © 2008 by Kelly Stephens

Cover design, Lorina Stephens. Copyright © 2008 by Lorina Stephens

Interior artwork remains the copyright of the individual copyright owners.

Published by Five Rivers Chapmanry www.5rivers.org
Manufactured in the U.S.A.
Published in Canada

This is a work of fiction and any resemblance to persons present or past is purely coincidental. All rights reserved. No part of this publication may be reproduced, stored in or introduced into a retrieval system, or transmitted in any form or by any means (electronic, mechanical, photocopying, recording or otherwise), without the prior written permission of both the copyright owner(s) and the above publisher of the book.

First Edition 2008

Library & Archives Canada/Bibliothèque & Archives Canada Data Main entry under title:

And the Angels Sang
Stephens, Lorina

ISBN 978-0-9739-2780-1

1. Title

Also by Lorina Stephens

Touring the Giant's Rib: A Guide to the Niagara Escarpment, Boston Mills Press

Credit River Valley, Boston Mills Press

Recipes of a Dumb Housewife, Lulu Publishing

Shadow Song, Lulu Publishing

Available through online booksellers worldwide
Select bookstores
Lulu Publishing: www.lulu.com
Five Rivers Chapmanry: www.5rivers.org

What follows is a collection of short stories written over the past 25 years. They are mostly, I've been told, hybrids, square pegs in a world of round holes, neither genre literature nor literary. A few in this collection were published in recognized periodicals; others were presented in workshops such as Clarion 1989, and OWWW (Other Worlds Writers' Workshop).

What are the stories of this anthology about? A writer writes what she knows. These stories are what I know. They are about people. They are about the human condition. They are about the inexorable and inevitable grey that colours our lives.

Some offer my own quirky slant on situations, because in the face of all the crumbling architecture of our world there is always a spark of hope, that impossible brazen daisy that grows through the cracks in the pavement. Other stories are flights of purest imagination, a result of asking the question: what if?

It is my sincere hope you will enjoy the journeys we are about to take together. If my stories have been a pleasure, or provocative, I welcome your feedback through my website (www.5rivers.org).

Lorina Stephens
September 2008

For Gary
as always

And the Angels Sang	1
Sister Sun	6
Have a Nice Day and Pass the Arsenic	14
Protector	24
The Gift	33
Over-exposed	41
Zero Mile	48
Darkies	56
A Case of Time	62
Jaguar	71
The Green Season	93
For a Cup of Tea	107
Summer Wine and Sweet Mistresses	124
Dragonslayer	130
Smile of the Goddess	143
A Dishwasher for Michelina	149
A Memory of Moonlight and Silver	162
Afterword	i

Figure 1: Watercolour and digital painting, Lorina Stephens

Figure 2 : Father Jean de Brébeuf
Metropolitan Toronto Reference Library / T-15468

And the Angels Sang

I have more pity for you than for myself; but sustain with courage the few remaining torments. They will end with our lives. The glory which follows them will never have an end.

Father Jean de Brébeuf, 1649

She is there again, that angel, sweet and yet like a siren, so beautiful it is deadly to look upon her. Once more it occurs to Father Jean de Brébeuf that she is as unlike an angel as he can imagine. She is dark, like a mahogany icon of the Virgin Mary. Unlike an icon this angel is fluid, alive. The song she sings hangs round him like incense and he feels delirious because of it

Somehow the song she sings is wrong, rather it isn't the song that is wrong but that she should sing it. Motets are reserved for the finer male choirs of the monastery. If the Cardinal were to discover her there would be trouble. The Cardinal disapproves of such things.

Still, her voice is breathtaking. The others are dissonant. Their rhythm is too intense, their enunciation slurred. Little is recognizable beyond their constant nasal whine. What language is that? Certainly it isn't French or Latin. It isn't even the language of his beloved Huron.

There is pain in his shoulders and he shrugs to relieve it. The pain intensifies. Best not to try that again. Likely the hair shirt abrades. Perhaps he shouldn't have been so zealous. Yet it is his fault the Iroquois had not accepted the gift of redemption he brought, his fault they turned upon the Hurons, their own brethren, and it is his fault the village of St. Louis lies in ruin, her people murdered, her hope destroyed.

He opens his eyes. For one clear moment he sees where he is and understands what is about to unfold. He finds the grace to say, "Let us lift our eyes to heaven at the height of our afflictions; let us remember that God is the witness of our sufferings, and will soon be our exceeding great reward." He tries with a force of will to push the haze from his thoughts, sees his friend, Paul Ragueneau, tied to the stake next to him, and smiles. But it is such an effort to smile, and he is so weary, so afraid.

Don't think of what causes fear. Thinking of that will dissolve his dark angel's music, its sweetness. Her voice can transport him to heaven and even epiphany. Yes, there, listen. That swelling sound above the cacophony of other voices, like a calling, rising, rising....

Oh, sweet Jesus, he prays, *if only Thou wilt let me rise to join Thee now, let me rise above these flames.* He tries to believe he is weightless, that if he has enough faith he will ascend to join that far, remote God whom he has served without surcease. He came to penetrate this endless, tormented wilderness for that God. Surely He will listen.

The Iroquois ring him like the flames they hold to him. He tries not to scream when the heat sears the tender flesh of his loins. He bites his tongue instead, tasting salt and copper.

Dear God, I am no longer a man, he thinks, and wonders if that will please the dark temptress who shrieks blasphemy at him.

Is it blasphemy his angel shrieks? Surely not. He strains to listen for her high, clear voice, ascending through the next complex series of notes. Lost in anticipation, he closes his eyes to distil the purity of the moment. There, yes, her voice lingers above him in the ribbed and vaulted ceiling, as the voices of all angels should.

Jubilato, she sings. *Joy indeed, sweet angel*, he thinks, *your music sweeps over me like baptism.*

Their baptism scalds. *God, what corruption is this? To baptize me with boiling water? Forgive them. Forgive her.* He refuses to scream aloud.

He opens his eyes to find her, that dark angel, to take her into his embrace and pardon her with what power he has. He would spare her from damnation. She is so young, so beautiful, so innocent.

Is it innocence that drives her to torment him so? Isn't it at her prompting that they baptize him in this cruel mockery?

If only the pain would stop. *Please, God, please, let it stop. Have I not served Thee faithfully?*

He closes his eyes to shut out the horror before him, to pull himself inward and deal with the waves of torment crashing over his body.

Pray you, sing, sweet angel, he thinks, *sing and we will all be transported.* He waits and she is silent. Only the chant of the Iroquois surrounds him.

To encourage her he tries to push his voice into song: *Twas in the moon of wintertime when all the birds had fled, that Mighty Gitche Manitou sent angel choirs instead.*

And the Angels Sang

His angel sings again, not his carol but the motet and again he feels the stillness of the cathedral around him. If only the others would settle into her song then all would be harmony.

How can there be harmony if she is singing in the cathedral? This is wrong. Dear God, forgive me for sinking into the pleasure of her voice. It is then he realizes it is she who has ordered that he be adorned with heated axe heads. He sees those glowing metal bits coming toward him. He hadn't wanted to see that. How can these people whom he has loved as his own inflict this agony upon him?

God, how can he endure this agony? *They burn, they burn, oh, God, how they burn!*

He feels himself become weightless the music is that sweet. He hears how his angel flies through the notes. *Damn the cardinal if he takes this angel from the choir. This is ecstasy. This is paradise.* Here, with his dark angel singing, there is no pain.

Lamb of God, take away the sins of the world.

He tries not to breathe, not to inhale the flames searing up his belly from the belt of pitch and resin with which they have girdled him.

My sin, he thinks, *I wear my sin,* and sees again the dark-eyed temptress who scorns him for spurning her. She shrieks lies about him. He wonders how he could think her voice sweet. It once had been so sweet, filling his head until his scalp tingled ... as it had that last time in the cathedral, when he received the Cardinal's blessing.

"May a host of angels follow you," the cardinal said. And Jean believed angels had. Somehow he made it through the forest, hadn't he? Somehow he gained admittance into Huron society. Surely only the angels could grant him that. Surely he had God's blessing, not just the Cardinal's. Surely God is watching now as his angel sings for her own life. Surely God hears the beauty of her song, the purity, painfully sweet—like the tingle of his scalp.

Nothing seems real as his angel takes his scalp from the warrior beside her. She shakes it high above her head, whooping as smatters of darkness splash across her face. When she brandishes the knife he had given her, he feels his heart will burst.

Suddenly the cathedral is silent. He can hear the wind outside - or is it inside? - the way it moans through the trees, the creak of boughs - benches? - as they shift and bend. Through a haze of tears he watches his angel and ignores the man who advances. Jean knows this warrior has his knife, her knife. He knows why the warrior approaches. He knows this as surely as he knows why his prayers are unanswered, why he must drink this bitter cup. This truth cuts him deeply.

He has heard from somewhere mortal wounds do not hurt. This must not be a mortal wound because he can feel the length of the blade in his chest. He knows now there is no cathedral but that of the green, indifferent forest. There are no angels here but the ones he wished. From a distance, where the silence and the pain have become one, he watches the warrior hold aloft a beating, bloody heart.

Jean says, or tries to say, he is not sure which, "Drink of it, all of you, for this is my blood of the covenant which is poured out for many for the forgiveness of sins."

And they drink. They eat. Again he hears his angel sing, joined now by others and he is light, the very essence of it. Now he knows. There is hell on earth. He is delivered of it.

Figure 3: Ink and brush painting, Lorina Stephens

Sister Sun

First published On Spec, *Fall 1993*

If he didn't find shelter soon he'd freeze. He hazarded one last glance around their observation post. A skin of ice had already formed on Lisa's tea. She'd even left her notes behind.

He sealed both hers and his in a pouch, shrugged into his parka and turned his back on six months. There was nothing left for him to do but survive until she forgave his sin and fetched him back to the present through the gate.

But, then, she might not. Why else would she have sabotaged life support?

He stepped outside. A monochrome landscape was before him, the sky too open, the stars too bright. The Inuit have over twenty names for snow. There was no subtle meaning in the snow for him. Cold. Killing cold. This was all it could ever mean.

At least the winter village was close. He'd head for the dance house and hope he wouldn't miss the mound of turf that was its roof. The girl might be there.

2

Man and woman - they work together well. They have to. The one called Lisa glances over at the one called Yukio, her fingers hovering over the keyboard.

"I didn't expect their language to be so evolved," she says.

Yukio grins and sets aside the pen. He dives through his holo of the whalebone spear, lands on his haunches and grunts. Lisa laughs, shrieks when he sets to pawing her.

"Oh, enough!" she says.

He stares at her closely, doing his best to imitate Neanderthal.

"Wrong time, dummy."

Yukio grunts again and lays his head against her breast.

"Poor, Yukio. Too much time spent in the past."

He makes a meaningfully pathetic noise and snuggles closer. Her breasts yield. She stiffens.

"We better get back to work," she says.

He withdraws, but she senses his reluctance.

For a long moment he watches her the way he would when they were children. "You're right," he says. "Ten months isn't a lot of time."

3

Warmth. He could only stand there and luxuriate in warmth. Vaguely, he sensed someone pulling the flap closed on the dance house, shutting this subterranean room from the long tunnel to the outside. There had been singing the moment he entered – a chant like a wheeze, the vibrating sound of a drum.

Now there was only warmth.

He opened his eyes.

Lisa would have been in raptures. There were eighteen adults here, three obviously elders, seven couples, a single man – perhaps recently come of age, perhaps a visitor from another village on a suit of marriage. The girl was here. He wondered if the boy had come for her.

Already the children tugged at their parents, demanding an answer to the question of his presence.

He stumbled around a few words. The elders slid glances to one another. Question there. Fear. He felt the sensibility of things tilt. The chant resumed. He sat near the tunnel door, dismissed, accepted. He may as well been off-planet for all their interest in him. Typical. Likely they thought him either a far-away hunter or one of the malevolent spirits that stalked their world. From the way the children watched him he suspected it was the latter.

That brought his attention back to the girl.

The girl paid him no notice. She knew already what kind of demon he was. Demons were best ignored. Her world was all for the young man. He'd be hunting with her family for the next two years if he was successful. He had no doubt the man would be. The furs he wore were luxurious. The attention he gave the girl was encompassing. The deference he showed her parents was exemplary.

The hunter would have her under his robes soon enough. And then his friend's. It was so easy for them to be promiscuous.

The story-chant ended. The girl bent to the old woman who led the last song. Whispers exchanged. The old woman nodded, sliding a worried glance to him. A drum vibrated once more and the girl danced, the old woman chanting. It took a few moments for the words to hit him. When they did that riot of emotions returned. Part of him bolted. Part of him sat there in horrid fascination while his sin transformed to legend before his eyes.

4

Yukio finds the girl on infrared - a fluke, a dot in a blizzard, lost no more than ten meters from the dance house tunnel.

"She'll die," Lisa says.

He mumbles in agreement.

"We can't just let her die!"

He turns to Lisa, frowning, watches the way light from the screen catches her cheek, the ends of her eyelashes, her upper lip. "We can't interfere. You know that."

"But she'll die."

He glances back at the screen, the dot that represents a fast-freezing life. Yes. The girl will die. Why does it matter to Lisa?

"We'd have to check with the department - "

"There isn't time," Lisa says.

He feels her move away. He turns. She's zippering into down coveralls. Panic jolts him. In the next moment he's beside her, his hands on her shoulders, his fingers dimpling her arms.

"You can't go out there."

She wriggles unsuccessfully, glares at him, brown eyes as cold as the wind outside. "I'm perfectly capable of taking care of myself."

"If you were you'd realize going out in zero visibility is foolish."

"I'm a big girl. I don't need your help anymore."

This is part of his panic, he knows: She doesn't need him anymore. Yukio, push my bike. Yukio, help me with this equation. Yukio, hug me. All those years of friendship. Growing together. Loving each other.

Loving her.

She stiffens, pulls away, something almost frightened in the way she looks at him.

He longs to draw her back, let his palms explore her. "Lisa, I - "

"Don't!"

Is that fear he sees? "I'm sorry, I - "

She backs to the wall.

"Lisa, I thought we - "

"It would be incestuous," she says.

His hands hang impotent at his sides.

"We're like brother and sister."

Anger takes him. "I'm not your brother."

He ignores the apologies she sputters, jams his legs into coveralls, yanks the zipper closed, slaps the tab shut. She implores him to listen, to understand. All he can understand is the years he's grown with her, known her, loved her.

The Arctic is unrelenting in its punishment when he steps outside, alone.

5

He was mesmerized by her dance, the way she moved, the way she mimed. The grandmother behind her chanted the tale well. It was all there. The girl had refined his sin to an art. He could do nothing but drown in legend: a girl in the dance house, the lamps blow out, darkness wraps and darkness hides, a man a man a man between her legs, a girl in the dance house, hands blackened, the lamps blow out, darkness wraps and darkness hides, a man a man a man between her legs.

She lay on the floor. He could feel the heat of his face, memory overlapping this scene. And still the legend filled his ears, defining why they'd accepted him so readily in the dance house, why they'd never bothered to question his presence.

A brother's back black, betrayal, betrayal, she cuts her breasts and throws them at him, Sister Sun hides from Brother Moon.

He could hardly breathe when she mimed the last scenes, hiding her face from an incestuous brother, a sun forever running from the moon. At that moment she stared at him, accusation and triumph.

He bolted. The chill air did nothing to freeze what he felt.

6

She sees him only as a blip that sketches a haphazard course on the screen to the other blip that is the freezing girl. Lisa guides him over the ear-transmitter and he can hear her, disturbingly intimate as compared to the howling wind. Already his face is numb. There's nothing to see but a cloud of snow. It's as if movement doesn't occur. He clings to the rope he attached to the observation post. Drop it and he will die. Like the girl, he could become lost within feet of shelter.

"Just a few more steps," Lisa says. "A little east."

She watches the blip shift. She has been unfair to him she thinks.

"Right there," she says.

He hears her urgency.

"You should be right on top of her."

He is. His boots collide with a pliable mass. His balance skews. He pitches forward. The girl groans. In his fall he's lost the rope.

"Yukio," Lisa says. "What is it?"

He says nothing. To tell her he's lost the rope would be to tempt fate. For a moment he senses the malevolence of the Arctic - all those spirits that torture the Inuit. He feels through the snow for the rope, his eyes filled with whiteness.

Lisa calls to him again. Her panic rises.

"Have you got her?"

"I'm with her."

"Come back," and she fears, for a moment, he won't, that he's lost the rope, that he's too cold already. What would she do without him? Yukio who has always been there?

He thinks where is it? Where is it? And finally finds it, loops it around his wrist and knots it, which is what he should have done in the first place, he knows.

"I have her," he says.

Lisa relaxes only slightly. He still has to carry the girl back. She watches two blips become one and then trace a laboriously slow path back to home.

When at last he stands within the outer lock he is iced with snow, the girl flung over his shoulder. Lisa feels the coldness of him as her arms close around him. He is safe. The girl is safe.

7

He turns from the holo when Lisa walks in. Her hair is towel-wrapped, her small figure swathed in a robe. He watches a bead of water slide round her neck, catch in the hollow of her throat and then slip, effortlessly, between her breasts.

"She's bathing," Lisa says.

"That wise?" he asks, a little rougher than he intended.

She sits on the chair next to him. "It's the best way I can think to get her body temperature up."

"She looks like you."

"Nonsense."

"Same eyes, same mouth, same cheekbones. She's even tiny like you."

Strange twist of nature, cruel coincidence.

"Some scientist."

Very scientific in fact. Ice bridges. An exodus of people who in the future would trace their lineage back to the oriental lands. "We should notify the department," he says. "Time interference—"

She leans toward him, touches his arm. "Please, Yukio."

He watches the trail that drop left, the way her robe parts as she leans toward him. His finger traces the dampness. He sees the woman now, not the girl, her mouth untasted, her skin so warm.

Her lips are cool beneath his, full. It amazes him how easy it is to bend to her, to taste. For a moment he relishes this thing he's waited to have. It is no more than a moment. A breath. She jerks back, anger rising.

"I'm not your brother," he says, and stalks from the room.

He finds himself at the bathroom of their small enclosure. Lisa's clothes are strewn across the floor, her bra dangling from the sink.

The girl lies in the tub, ivory against white, steaming water to her chin. Her breasts glisten where they are exposed, the nipples dark and swollen, jet hair like ribbons. She does nothing. She only lies there in the steam, the dark sea goddess the Inuit fear so greatly.

He fears her. She resembles Lisa very much.

He steps into the room. His heart beats so hard he wonders why it doesn't echo from the walls.

Her eyes open. She stares at him. There is nothing of fear in her. She watches him, her eyes moving slowly, slowly, down his length. Her arms rise, hands rippling over the water and then cup her breasts. She smiles. Accusation and triumph.

He thinks only of Lisa when he kneels beside her and sucks upon one of the breasts she offers him, slides his hands into the heat of the water, lifts her dripping. He lets her go long enough to strip. Her body is slippery, hot to his touch when he presses himself, naked, against her. She makes a little leap when he lifts her buttocks into his palms, her legs around him. She moans when he enters her.

Lisa. Lisa like this, tiny, wet, breasts fleshy against his chest, thighs firm around his waist. Lisa with whom he's grown. Lisa to whom he makes love. Lisa....

...who finds them fucking, his fingers biting deeply into the girl's ass, her head hung back and dripping, moans in her throat, Yukio in her body. Yukio.

She hurls her bra at him. "Eat this, you bastard!" And flees.

8

For four days Lisa has not spoken to him. And for four days the blizzard has prevented him from releasing the girl back into the primitive cold that is so much a part of her life.

Finally the blizzard does abate, enough that he can let the girl out, be sure she will find her way back to the winter village. He watches her go on the screen. She turns back to look. He punches in the camouflage code. A look of surprise crosses her face. She turns. She runs into a world of twilight white.

For awhile he listens on audio. Such quiet out there. And then the wolves howl.

Lisa, who sits beside him, speaks.

"How could you?"

What should he answer, he wonders, and says nothing.

The wolves continue to howl.

9

He wakes with a start, aware that he is cold, shivering. He swings his legs over the cot.

"Lisa," he calls, and then feels the quiet.

He rises, pulls on trousers, sweaters, pushes his feet into shoes.

When he enters the workroom he knows where Lisa is. The environmental controls have all been sabotaged, his link to the department back in the 22nd century destroyed.

Heat shoots through his chest – adrenaline. The word marooned jumps in his mind.

His gaze moves to Lisa's cup. A skin of ice is forming on the tea. If he doesn't find shelter soon he'll freeze.

10

He has no idea how long he has walked. Sister Sun rose and set in two hours, chased by Brother Moon who shines pale and cold upon an Arctic night. The gate is close – an inuksuk older than any legend the Inuit remember, a cairn of rocks over twenty feet tall.

He reaches the granite rocks that resemble a giant man, sets his back to the inuksuk and slides down. The transmitter in his parka spews out a stream of static. He bites off his mitten, flicks the switch off, shoves his hand back into cover.

If they are to find him he will have to depend on Lisa.

Wolves howl in the distance. The first glimmer of an aurora waves on the horizon, flashes and then erupts into curtains of green, blue and red.

He lifts his head and howls. The wolves answer.

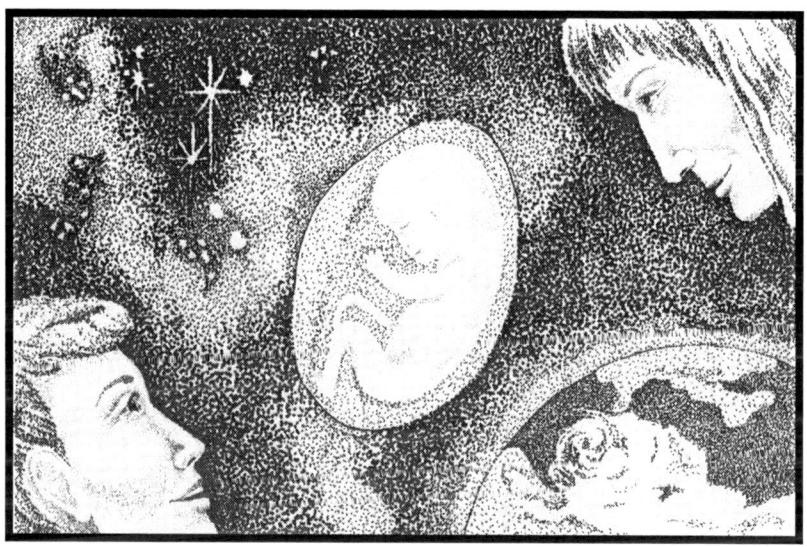

Figure 4: Pen & ink sketch, Lorina Stephens, previously published, Beyond…, 1990

Have a Nice Day and Pass the Arsenic

Published previously Beyond..., *1990*

Doc told me I'd adjust. Lying bastard. It's so easy to be an expert from an armchair.

I could see nothing but his face as I worked, hear nothing but his voice in the drone of data from the traffic computers.

A freighter blipped on the hologram in front of me. The sound of it was like a foetal heartbeat. The holo blurred. I couldn't help it.

What a stupid time to cry.

Three weeks after I'd shipped back out to Lunar spaceport I thought I'd eat the next person I saw. Boss had raked me good. One more outburst of anger and I'd lose my rec privileges. If I lost my rec, those tranquil hours in the arboretum, I'd really be of no use to Boss or myself. It was just so hard to forget that I'd failed.

Again Doc's patronizing voice slipped through me, ghostly, haunting, as if I'd never forget.

"It's all right, Angie. You miscarried. That doesn't mean you failed."

Doc was still a lying bastard. What did he know about carrying a child inside you and then losing it, especially a child you've carried almost to term?

"Answer them, Nealie!"

My gaze shot to Kyran who sat at control station three. Stations two and four were plugged into their work. Nice quite types. Not like Kyran.

Had she said something?

"Answer them!" she repeated.

Only now I heard the freighter's captain, the person Kyran was telling me to answer. I flinched. I didn't mean to, but I did, my hand crashing down to the com-board.

"Stuff it!" I shot back at Kyran. She rolled her eyes, that smug look on her face. Boss would hear about this, I was sure. Kyran had been bucking for my position as head controller for months. The only way to save my skin was to save this moment.

I opened my channel to the freighter. "You're heading fine, Zero-Niner-One. Docking permission for Cargo Bay Three, over."

"Acknowledged, Lunar. Docking at Cargo Bay Three, over."

"That's twice this shift," Kyran said.

"You keeping score?"

"Call in a replacement."

"I don't need to."

"I think you do."

"That's not your decision to make."

"Neither should it be yours."

"Fine. File your damned observation. We'll let Boss decide."

That, also, had been a stupid thing to do - to encourage Kyran to file a grievance against me. I didn't need Boss to find out about this.

I kept my eyes upon the traffic holo and for a time I managed to keep my attention sharp. Doc's voice kept intruding. After while I saw little of the holo. All I could think of was the three year's pay I'd spent for AI privileges. Sure I could save for another three years, live that life of austerity again, but there was no more time for me. The Artificial Insemination Board would refuse my application after this year. I'd be too old. No other way of looking at it. Even the low-risk of bearing and birthing in Lunar spaceport's low gravity wouldn't do me any good. My body had betrayed me. My body and time.

Kyran almost had to jolt me again, but another blip on the holo alerted me. This incoming traffic was nothing like I'd ever seen before. This was no freighter. This was enormous, ponderous in its enormity. And then it hit me. The blip on my holo was a long-haul tin. Rare. They never came in this close to Earth. Usually the Martian port handled them, unless it was a tin that had gone intergalactic.

My hands were shaking when I punched up visual on the ship. It was sleek, long, like a silver cigar void-bound. None of the usual towers and appendages hung like crystalline spikes from its body. This was as efficient as it got, even down to the crew. When it had left Earth-system, a pregnant woman would have piloted this tin. Her child would pilot it back. Cryogenics and computers took care of the rest.

Something in my chest smouldered. I tried to quench it but it wouldn't die: the woman aboard this ship was coming in so close to Earth because she *had* been intergalactic and it was her turn for AI, a necessity to have another captain in her womb before the tin turned around. The AIB wouldn't concern themselves with her age. It was quite acceptable for them to allow her a child, even though that child would never have a playmate, never

Have a Nice Day and Pass the Arsenic

know what sun or wind or cold would feel like. I could give a child that. *She* couldn't.

What made it even harder to swallow was that might have been me coming in for docking. I'd been through the whole drill, got my intergalactic wings and at the last minute backed out. It was a child I wanted. Not a pilot to take my ship back to Earth.

"This is Lunar spaceport," I managed to say. "Please identify yourself, over."

"This is the *Onandatta* ... Delta-Fiver-Two, Captain Pharady sp-speaking. Requesting permission to dock."

I waited a moment for her to signal *over*. The stilted cadence of her speech caused me to wonder if she spoke much, if she were unsure how to coordinate sound, lips and tongue. How would she keep the skills of communication sharpened? Who would she have to talk to out there? It would have been years past that her mother died.

Finally the pause in our dialogue led me to believe she'd finished.

"Your cargo, Baker-Fiver-Two, over?" I asked, needing to know that information before I could assign her to one of the three bays capable of taking her.

"Fresh water," she answered.

Fresh water. Such irony that. There'd be nothing fresh about the water in this tin's holds. It would be as stale as a whore in a spaceport.

I scanned the bays available to receive her, signalled one to prepare and then: "You're clear to dock at Cargo Bay 112, over."

"Cargo B-bay 112. Acknowledged."

There was nothing to do now but wait until she'd been sealed at her bay. I was watching that procedure while shuffling over smaller traffic when the whole damned station shuddered like I'd never felt it shudder before. It was the *Onandatta* docking. I thought that was it. No more worries about trying to get pregnant, about trying to stay out of Boss's temper. I'd be just another blob of garbage floating around with the sludge in Sewer's Way. Distantly, I was aware of one of my team swearing.

The station didn't shatter. To my surprise Captain Pharady of the *Onandatta* signalled me again, this time on a visual. She wasn't what I expected. There was this elongated thing staring at me in the holo, all loose-limbed and lanky, her skin pale, almost glass-like, hair which was thin, white, incredibly long. It was her eyes that stopped me from making some cryptic remark. They were warm, brown, like sienna pools with glints of gold. Anyone with eyes like that wasn't all bad. I couldn't take out my frustration on her.

"Thang you, Controller."

That was it. That was all she said before turning away.

"It's Nealie. Angie Nealie," I blurted out, wanting to stop her. "Have a nice day, eh?"

As soon as I said that – have a nice day – I cringed. What an inane, dumb thing for a person to spout, especially to someone who's just finished half a lifetime of space-travel. Maybe it was just my frustration and the pressure of this shift. Not long and I'd be off duty. Even at this moment the control-room lights were dimming, shifting to a golden glow to simulate sunset.

Pharaday halted, sharply, as if my stupid statement had been a rope and snared her. She turned, those eyes sharp with question, her face screwing up into something that reminded me of a pale prune.

"Day?" she asked.

I didn't answer for a moment, not understanding her question.

"Day?" she said again. "I'm sorry. I don't understand. Was I to reply?"

I watched her, the way the station's slight gravity let her lift, like a kite catching an errant breeze.

"Reply to what?" I asked. All I wanted to do was sign out, have dinner, relax in the arboretum while the children there soothed my grief. I hoped this situation wasn't going to drag on.

"Have a nice ... *day*?" she asked.

"Sure. Yeah."

Now she really looked perplexed, her face zooming toward the holocamera. "Day! What does it mean to own a day?"

Something inside me felt as if it were draining to a puddle on the floor. I guess I must have looked pretty dull-normal to her because she stammered out her question again. By now, Kyran barbed me with sharp looks.

Blessed virgins! How was I to explain about a day? I knew that on Earth the sun appeared to come up; you got up; you spent maybe eight to ten hours working at full jets and then the sun appeared to slide down the opposite horizon. Eventually you wound down too.

That was a day.

But Phraday's standards, reference points, weren't the same at all. In her can there wouldn't be any day/night simulation. There was no need. She'd been born in space. It was efficient to save the energy that could create that day/night effect. To her the sun, any sun, was an unpleasant, unromantic star of white, yellow, blue, red, brown, black. Her world was a void through which things streaked.

What was a day to her?

"It's not important," I finally said and blanked the holo with a punch at the board.

There was body-heat at my back – my relief controller. I didn't bother to swing around in greeting. What would be the use when she and Kyran were probably exchanging grimaces? My fingers found the sign-out key, jabbed it. I left wordless.

Usually I'd pick something up for dinner from the commissary, go home, eat, shower and spend the evening in the arboretum. Some habits are hard to break. Tonight would be no different.

I was splashing in the shower when I thought of Pharaday again. She'd be heading Earthside. A rendezvous with motherhood. For a moment I stared at the shampoo in my hand, the scent of herbs and flowers twisting round my mind. I mashed it into my hair, scrubbing as if I could shampoo my grief away.

The entry bell chimed. Terrific timing. I just kept on scrubbing. It chimed again, one over the other like a hiccough of sound. I swore, slammed the water-flow off and wrapped a towel around my body, cursing my curiosity. If I didn't find out who this was, I'd spend the rest of the evening wondering.

The shampoo was dripping into my eyes when I checked the security screen. I froze. The goose-bumps on my skin tightened, making more goose-bumps. I shivered.

"Please, Nealie. Let me in."

It was Pharaday. Her face was a mask of worry, her soft eyes shifting, checking the corridor.

What was she doing here?

I didn't think when I let her in, blinking away shampoo, cursing that it smarted. When the door hissed shut behind her she pressed her back to it.

"I'm sorry to do ... this to you, Nealie. I need your help."

Shock still sealed my voice. I mouthed a silent *me?*

"I've missed the sh-shuttle to Earth."

I pulled the towel closer. "So catch the next one."

Her pale brow furrowed. I couldn't help but think of wrinkled glass.

"You don't understand," she said.

"I guess I don't."

"I have to stop ... inspection of my ship."

My gaze narrowed on her. "You doing something illegal?"

She nodded.

"Contraband?"

She shook her head.

"I'm not about to stick my neck out for nothing."

"You could stop the inspection," she whispered. "You have that ... authority."

"I still need to know why I should do that."

"I don't want the cryogenic units checked."

Units? As far as I knew that word should have been singular.

"You better explain," I said.

"There's someone on b-board I need to ... get Earth-side."

I reached for the door release, thinking of my last session with Boss. "I'm not in the business of smuggling."

Her hand touched my shoulder, briefly, withdrew. "I'll offer you whatever you want – money. Lots of money. More than you could make in ... four years."

Four years worth of wages. That could buy me an appointment with AIB. I had until the end of the year.

But human smuggling?

"I'll let you know," I said, letting the door swish open.

Her face screwed up. "Not much t-time. Two hours and they'll finish ... clearing cargo. Then inspection of i-interior."

The door closed. She still stood in my home. I couldn't let her hang around out in the station.

"Sit," I said. "I'm going out. I have to think."

In moments I had the shampoo cleared from my hair, was dressed and striding into the arboretum. The sound of children's laughter accented birdsong, all of it like a sweet hymn of contentment. A bench brought me to observation. None of the children minded that I watched them in their play. They were accustomed to my silent participation. When they had need of me for a magic kiss to heal a scrape, or for a sympathetic listener or an excited sharer they would join the dominion of my bench.

As I watched them dive round the trees, Pharaday's urgency melted from my mind. What could be more important than these moments? – the carolling of their laughter, their shouts of combat, the smell of their sweaty bodies ... like dust and excitement mixed into one sweet melange.

One of the girls rushed up to me, flinging her exquisite body into my arms.

"I want a hug, Angie," she panted, her breath moist against my throat.

On instinct my arms closed round her, double, like wings around a fledgling. I found I couldn't breathe. Such tightness in my chest. How could I adjust to a life without this?

Doc was still a lying bastard.

Gently, I pushed my little friend to arm's length, blinking away the blur from my eyes.

"Hug enough?" I asked.

She nodded, dark eyes sparkling and then she darted away. Something about her reminded me of a hummingbird – zooming in for a dip of nectar, zooming away, a faerie in flight. My knees were weak when I stood. Pharady was very much on my mind. She offered me something I couldn't refuse.

I made no preamble when I stepped through the door of my room. My fingers were on the com-unit before Pharaday was on her feet.

"Nealie here," I said, contacting Cargo Bay 112. "I don't want that tin scrubbed down yet. There's the possibility of a virus onboard."

"We've had no word from med," the tech answered.

"Pharaday didn't show for an Earthside shuttle. She was exhibiting symptoms of a void-type bacterium."

That was enough to convince the tech. She acknowledged, barking orders to her crew even before our com-link snapped off.

I turned back to Pharaday who stood there with tears in her eyes.

"I'm grateful ... s-so grateful," she kept murmuring.

"Don't be grateful yet. I want to know just what I've stuck my neck out for."

Pharaday slumped to the chair. "My daughter."

"Your what?"

"My daughter."

It was my turn to find some support. I eased to the edge of the desk, ran a hand through my hair as if that might settle my shock.

"Your daughter?" I finally asked.

She nodded.

"What did you do? Have a fling in space?"

She shook her head.

It fell on me then just exactly what she'd done. This was the original captain I was looking at. God only knew how old she was. How desperate had she been to keep herself in hyb, to risk building a cryo unit out of spare parts?

I knew only too well how desperate she'd have been. I would have done exactly the same thing.

"They'll hunt you," I said. "Your daughter's company property."

"She's mine," she hissed

That was something I really couldn't argue with.

"What do you expect to do?" I asked. "Just walk away from here – daughter and all?"

"I thought I'd stow away on the shuttle bound for Earth, go north, maybe the sub-Arctic."

"They'll track you like hot meat."

"There has to be somewhere!"

I wondered at that. Why couldn't there be somewhere for a mother to have a haven with her child? Was it so wrong of her to want to get to know her daughter? Was it unnatural?

As far as I was concerned there was a place for Pharaday and her daughter. I'd make it for them.

The easiest thing I've ever done was to contact Boss and tell her I was taking two weeks medical leave. She only smiled and punched in her consent. By the time I was heading for Cargo Bay 112 - Pharaday, dressed in a helmeted scrub-suit, on my heels - I'd booked passage on the next Earth shuttle which was due to leave in six hours.

There were a few tense moments before we entered the bay. A team in search of Pharaday had stopped us for questions. Quick thinking and a little deceit helped. Adrenaline was till thumping through my limbs when I juggled the clearance and surveillance circuits at the bay and stepped into the quarantined area.

It felt odd to enter a long-haul tin again, odd as if I'd gone back ten years, my wings all golden and sharp at my breast. This ship felt just as ominous, enormous as my test ship had. For a moment I wondered if I could go through with this. What I felt must have been obvious. Pharaday asked if I'd ever flown.

I shrugged. "Test flights."

"You're not th-thinking of - ."

"Just do what I say and I'll get you and your daughter to safety."

I left her scrambling in my wake.

The first place I headed was the hyb section where I set up the program to bring her daughter out of deep freeze. It all came back so easily. Perhaps too easily. Pharaday kept batting me with questions until I sat her into a med chair and immobilized her with acupuncture. When I started rearranging her face and switching our genetic records, her eyes spoke only too clearly of her understanding ... and of her gratitude, gratitude I felt I didn't deserve. Pharaday was giving me the opportunity to taste motherhood. My motives weren't entirely noble.

When we strapped ourselves into the shuttle Earthbound, our ruse went well enough. As for her daughter - she was old enough that we dressed her up as a hooker. For the majority of people up here, hookers weren't worth notice.

She and her daughter made it to their northern retreat without a lot of problems. I'd made sure to have my credit converted to cash for her - no trail that way. As for me? There are moments I still find it difficult to look in a mirror. It's Pharaday's who stares back at me. I've often wondered if she feels the same, as if when we traded faces and identities we'd traded our souls as well. Maybe that's what Pharaday meant when she replied to my dumb statement of *have a nice day* when we parted. She told me to pass the arsenic. Maybe we were killing a little bit of our lives by doing what we did. Maybe we were going on to that life beyond. Who knows?

My daughter is growing strong and straight ... terribly long because of weightlessness. Thinking of stealing sperm from the AIB as Pharaday gives me pleasure. I beat the system.

In another two hours we'll be leaving the *Onandatta* in the life-sled. There's a nice little moon in a cluster of moons down there that's supposed to be a good place to farm – no questions asked, mothers and daughters welcome. The SOS to the company has started. With luck they'll only find space-dust.

Doc's still a lying bastard. I never did adjust.

Figure 5: Watercolour, pen & ink, Lorina Stephens

Protector

Did you know only about two percent of the population are categorized as Protectors? Rare people. Rare way of thinking. We're hardwired, according to Jungian and Myers-Briggs theory, to be gentle, caring, to avoid conflict and attempt to bring order into chaos. And a little deep-trance therapy goes a long way to reinforcing those psychological fundamentals.

Sitting here in this closet, uncomfortable on the lumpy shoes, I'm wondering what order I can bring to this world I know? How can I affect positive change for others when I see nothing but chaos in how society chooses to use my talents? If we're so blessedly rare, then why use us in this manner?

And why am I a stow-away in a closet, refugee from the cold and bitter storm outside? In another life I would have thrown my own shoes in this closet, found comfort in the familiar surroundings of home. In another life Mother might have made me safe. Might have. Likely not. There was so much pride when she said, "Julia, girl, it's an honour to be called as a Protector."

An honour indeed. Such honour to sit on shoes in the darkness of a closet not mine, the rank smell of feet my laurel crown. An honour to depend upon the largess of people who want only to unburden themselves of pain, sorrow, guilt. The companion without recourse. Rare we may be, but both Protector and Pariah because of our difference.

Still, I could accept this closet as home for the remainder of my life. A closet could make a home. Why not? Better this than the refrigerator carton I'd called home for two nights, odd bit of irony that. I'd slept shuddering against the knifing wind, my bones shattering with pain not just from cold but because of the woman in the house who suffered from arthritis. She knew I'd accept that pathetic bit of shelter, and I paid for my room with her pain.

It's what I do, you see. It's my raison d'être. And they, the ones who have need of that last recourse of a Protector, know how to lure us. We aren't rewarded with bricks and mortar as wages for taking the sins of the world.

To grant us status with these gifts would be censure of the very fabric of a society that has created need of us.

And so I shift on the shoes, hoping I won't be found, hoping whatever ills are in this house won't find me, at least until I can rest, perhaps steal some food and then my way back out into the streets where I can fold myself into the dark spaces. Maybe, just this once, they'll leave me be, let me lap at the warmth this closet can afford. I won't bother the owner. I won't ask for food. I won't beg. Just let me sit on these shoes, alone in my warmth and the silence.

I almost laugh at the absurdity of it; I live in a world full of people and I'm totally alone. No one wants to keep a Protector. Just use them and let them go. It's folly to think I won't have to pay for this respite. They'll use me too soon. They'll find me.

I reach through the closet with my senses, groping for that ripple that will tell me if a Protector's needed here. I hear before I feel. Shoes scuffing the carpet. My pulse goes off like cannon. The air lurches. His disease leaps toward me. Suddenly not even the darkness is enough concealment. Will he find me? Will he hurt me?

I chew on a sob. In my mind I can see shoed feet lift and fall in the hall outside the closet. The shoes are black, leather, an Oxford-style. The feet in them are covered in grey wool socks. Of course the socks would be wool. The temperature has been sub-zero for days.

I remember the cold, the memory of it as frigid as reality. Just blend in with the shoes. Old shoes. Shoes no one wants. That sounds luxurious – not to be wanted. Just thinking of being wanted leaves a place inside me utterly still, as if moving would trip the trap.

I clutch at the crucifix at my breast.

Mother wanted me fifteen years ago. She wanted me to be a Protector. Such a convenient way to fluff her feathers for the neighbours. *What does your daughter do? Why, she's a Protector.*

Did it matter my wishes? No. Just as it doesn't matter now. My wishes are irrelevant. I'm a Protector, a freak of psychological genetics, and in the scheme of Darwinian theory it is what the rest of my parish wishes that's important. Use me they may, but they will at least keep me from death. Their compassion for Christ was little better than what they afford me. At least they crucified him for all the good he did.

And now I want to hide. The last person was more than I wanted to face. There comes a point of saturation. Surely someone must realize this?

No. Doubtful that. To understand a Protector you must be a Protector. I am alone. I have my assigned parish from which I cannot escape, though I have tried. As God is my witness, I have tried. And still I accept their pain. It's a compulsion.

I realize a hopeful fact: the man walking near me must be wealthy. He's wearing wool socks. Wool is a rare commodity, result of the reduction of grazing animals. This person can buy anything.

Wool socks! Imagine that!

I want to laugh with relief.

I choke on the laugh. Pain hits me hard in the stomach. Horrible, suffocating pain. I should never have left the street. I should have never walked through that open door. Stupid! Stupid! Stupid! Don't I know by now an open door is an invitation?

I retch. There's nothing in my gut to throw up. My heaving is dry, harsh.

Damn you! I want to scream at the passing man.

My curse is unheard, unsaid. They never hear me anyway. That's my job, the hearing part. That's what they tell me I'm supposed to do. Hear for the entire stinking world. I've been hearing for fifteen years.

And feel. I've always been great at feeling. Now I feel for them all. A modern day healer. Deliverer of happiness. No pain for anyone. Happiness is a right. The pain, the despair is all mine.

Lucky me.

I hold my breath, gulp. God, what does he have?

I don't want to tell him it's okay. I don't want his bloody pain. I'm trapped. He'll know I'm in the closet, hiding. He'll know because his pain will lessen. The door will open and he'll smile, relieved, his arms stretching out as if to embrace me with his sickness.

Enough! I want to scream. But don't, and agony crashes over my skin, red waves rushing from my mouth, smashing against my breast, foaming across my toes. The darkness is mired in red.

A laugh like a sigh. I can hear him laugh. It makes me feel worse to hear the relief in his voice. The closet handle creaks, metal on metal, and the door swings out, sweeping in light.

I squint my bloodshot eyes. Everything is black and white. Black bulk of a man. White like a corona around him. His arms raise, parting the whiteness, creating eddies that sharpen into blackness dripping past his knees. Another kind of whiteness cracks his face. It is like staring into headlights.

"I knew you'd come," he says.

The wall is hard against my back, refusing to admit me, my knees aching where they press against my chest. My teeth are biting the pain in my stomach. His pain. If only he'd go away. If only I could melt into this wall.

But too late. He scoops me off his shoes. I must be very light because he moves me so easily. To me it feels as if my stomach is eating its way out through my spine; all I can taste is bile.

The comfort in his arms is meant solely for himself. They are large, soft. I can do nothing to stop his caress. His pain in my body has predetermined that. In the end he takes me to his bed, tucks me against him and sleeps. It is likely the first sleep of peace he's had in months. As a Protector I know he needs this. I know he needs to be reassured by the presence of another human being, someone to share the reality. And distantly I wonder what it would be like to be loved.

I finger the crucifix. How could You love them when You'd never known love Yourself? Show me!

When his breathing deepens and his limbs slacken, I haul my stiff legs over the edge of the bed which is the softest thing I've known in a very long while. Survival instinct keeps me going. Only barely. I don't think they counted on it wearing out, otherwise they would have realized a Protector can still commit suicide. They need me to live. I wonder if it ever occurred to them to consider if I wanted to live.

There's enough of survival left to make me steal some clothes, big as they are, from the floor and the closets. A brown leather wallet dumps out of his trousers. I watch it unfold on the carpet by my bare feet. I bend, clutch the wallet into my hands and furtively, glancing at his snoring face, open the thing. I look at a sheaf of plastic cards and actual currency which is difficult to comprehend. I let the wallet drop back to the floor, afraid. This money is something that will do me no good. I won't be able to use it. No one will accept it. I buy my privileges with pain.

Again I bend to his clothes. A face in the bureau mirror arrests me. I freeze somewhere between kneeling and standing.

Such a wild face, dark eyes glittering, dark hair askew around a face as pale and fragile as ice. Bones stretch the skin to a veneer.

My fingers tremble as I touch the glass, a kamikaze girl looking in a haunted mirror.

Is this me? I remember a girl who pulsed with health the way the sun pulsed with light.

His down jacket flaps loosely around me when I reach the street. The snow is exceptionally bitter tonight, maybe because I was warm for just a little while. I shrug deeper into the coat. At least the rats in my stomach have died.

Time to wander again, to search for a quiet haven, no people, no pain. I wonder if Christ felt like this. Was that what he meant in Gethsemane? Father, let this cup pass.

Let this cup pass.

The crucifix at my breast is sharp with cold, a reminder of the modicum of pain I must accept. It's a comforting thought. I won't face the cross, not like Him. I'm not sure I could be that noble, that brave, that selfless to die for all these unhearing people. If only they'd listen to themselves, each taking, each giving, letting pain and pleasure balance. I'd be free.

At this time of night the street is quiet, the row-houses like cardboard cut-outs in the dim light of the lamps. The only movement is in the endless curtain of snow that drifts and sways in any errant breeze. I like this silent scene. No people. No demands. No Protector needed here. It could be like this forever. But, no. Nothing's changed in over two millennia.

For now, however, the silence is a benediction.

I remember feeling like this when I was a kid in school, enjoying the odd quiet lunch that would come my way. It would be so utterly pleasant not to listen to someone's most recent heartbreak, not to be called upon for sage advice, not to be asked to relieve the pain. Take two aspirin and call me in the morning times.

How was I supposed to know what to do? They didn't want to hear the truth. They only wanted relief. A bandage received from my nodding head.

And then came the selection and the days of endless deep-psych therapy. The latest in medical technology. A listener, a Protector for every community. What did it matter that I hurt for them all? I'd been doing it all my life anyway, they told me.

Suddenly I want to have a quiet lunch. This lack of feeling is addictive. If I were to go to the clinic for my weekly check-up would they give me therapy to rid me of this feeling? In all of this world surely there must be one, small place I can claim as my own, a place no one else needs, a place I am not needed. I'm out of bandages!

My path is now circuitous; I know the town better than its planners, and so I go to the backwater streets where there will be no action. Quiet, residential streets where the likelihood of being caught is slim. The windows I pass blaze like orange fires, sometimes smudged by the smoky haze of TV screens. Here there are mostly childhood maladies, overworked muscles, the odd migraine. My senses stay alert to anyone afflicted with something chronic, terminal, to the pains of despair, loneliness.

Isolation from these urban lives bothers me less and less as the snow mounts. Isolation is safety.

As I wade through the storm, I wonder if other Protectors are as lonely as I. I wonder how they deal with the emotional pains. That is the worst. Physical pains, well, they're something real. The emotional pains – sometimes I've found myself cringing against the bricks, terrified for hours to move, and then realized I'd taken someone else's fear to myself. It might be heartening to hear how others manage. It would be nice to have someone to listen to me, a nodding head bandaging my wounds.

That would only increase their burdens as Protectors. I couldn't do that. And so I listen to myself.

By now I've made fair progress, although I'm getting colder and there's a cavern where my stomach was. The snow is now ribbons instead of curtains. Every now and then the moon's gloom touches my face.

Ahead are the rail yards, full of empty cars that will afford me the luxury of isolation. I almost dare to hope. It's something I haven't done since entering my profession. As I trudge over the rails I have flash-backs, moments of the deep-psych trance, words and music spilling over and over in my mind like the steady drip of water. I remember hearing Bach's cantata 147.

> *Drink of joy from deathless springs.*
> *Theirs is beauty's fairest pleasure;*
> *Theirs is wisdom's holiest treasure.*

Is it blasphemous of me to think that somehow these verses were perverted?

My legs are burning with cold by the time I haul myself into a cattle car. The smell of old cow urine is warming, earthy, real. Drawn by that comfort I slouch into a corner and wait for my ride to take me out, away to who knows where in my parish? Just as long as it isn't here.

I dig into my pockets for the bit of sausage and cheese I pilfered. There was no need, really, for me to have stolen. I would have been given whatever food I wanted, often left on a doorstep, a shed, offerings to the Protector in the way offerings have been left for spirits throughout history. Those offerings, however, were given with the same intent as those of history, a form of payment for a solicited service, and sometimes I just wanted to close my doors to trade.

Later, when I curl into myself for warmth, I curse myself again for not stealing that man's socks. I fall into sleep thinking about grey wool.

It's dawn before the car shunts, banging me out of sleep. It's a dreary day, winds as fitful as my sleep had been, great globs of snow slopping between the slats of the car. They make gritty puddles on the dun floor. I rub the sand out of my eyes and wet from my nose.

For awhile I'm rocked in my sanctuary as cars are strung into a strand. There's nothing to do but brace myself into the corner, clutching to hope.

I'm almost giddy with hope. Maybe it's the hunger that's making me giddy. I should have accepted offerings.

And then the car makes one enormous lurch. I'm going! Out! Away! Maybe there is hope for me in this parish. Tears chill my cheeks and then I sleep, swaying in my clattering cradle.

A change in scent awakens me. The air streaming through the car is now fragrant with the smell of trees. It excites me. It's such a healthy smell.

I lean toward the swaying wall, the clack of metal wheels on metal rails a steady percussion. A blur of white and green streams between the slats, sealed with a gash of blue that is utterly pure. This must be the colour of death. Something infinite, simple.

My excitement pushes me to ram open the car door. It rumbles away. I crouch at the opening, my fingers clamped to the boards. Cold stings my face, slices through my hair and fills my world. I breathe. Coldness so clean it aches in my lungs. My nose feels as though it's been glued shut.

I'm drowning in a world of my own feelings, and I relish this drunkenness.

The landscape is stark, made only of white, green and blue. There are no signs of any civilization here. That's like an introduction and, without thinking, I walk the air for a heartbeat and then puff into a ravine of white. My world spins around in a topsy-turvy whirl of sensation. Finally I stop. The train is only motion in the distance. The skin on my wrists and ankles flames from the cold.

I laugh, silently at first, then aloud, listening to my voice disappearing in the trees.

I've escaped! Oh, God, but this feels good!

It isn't long before I stagger to my feet. I hazard a glance to the opposite hill, the hill that will take me farther away from the rails and civilization, and realize it is both higher and longer than I thought. Pines grow out of it like furry, green mushrooms. The lure of that quietude is too inviting. I turn my back to the rails and begin to wade.

By the time I have a firm hold halfway up, I'm more battered than I'd have been being civilization's Protector. My climb has cost me four tumbles back to the valley, one of which scraped open my cheek when I slammed into a trunk. My fingers are raw, numb and bleeding because I'd lost my gloves on one of those tumbles. The cold is without compassion.

I will rest for a little while.

There are flashes of blue over my head. Birds, I think, with crested heads and raucous voices that scream *jay, jay, jay*. Another creature like a red jewel preens in a branch just out of arm's reach. Its beak opens and I am overcome with music. Surely I could be happy in a world like this.

The bird continues to warble its high, clear song, tugging at something in my chest. This is so good. I feel guilty I should have come to a place where I can feel this good. I'm not supposed to feel good. That's a feeling reserved for those who have used me.

"Stop!" I squawk at the singing thing. "Stop!"

It flaps away without thought of my pain. No Protector here for me.

The time has come to move. Already my legs have stiffened. They move like sticks. By now I have learned to make my ascent by lunging from tree to tree, grasping on, resting and then lunging once again. In this fashion I reach the summit by the time the sun is setting. My face is turned toward the endless gloom of the forest, standing trunk on trunk, an infinite ocean like all those to whom I have listened and healed for fifteen years. I realize I may freeze out here. There will be no carton shelter, no shed left open to insulate me from this raw world.

Even quiet lunches cost.

I can't help it. Panic rises. I feel the sickness of it under my tongue. In the distance I can hear the long-away whine of a train horn. I whirl, my hair slapping against my face.

It's too dark in the pines to see my way now. Heedless of the danger, I pitch back toward the valley, sliding, sending up fountains of snow as I go. My heart's pounding so violently I can feel its pressure against my stolen coat. There are plumes of breath streaming over me.

I've lost my way. I careen to a halt at a precipice that overlooks the tracks and my earlier place. I notice a blasted tree not far from where I'd been. It's directly below me, some eighteen feet or so. The train isn't far and I must get to it. Perhaps every kind of survival has its prices.

I leap, reaching for the Y of the tree's branches. My fall is too rapid. I can do nothing to change my course. Too late I see a third branch aiming for my belly.

For a moment I think of that man's pain, the bloody, red pain.

I am aware only of my own pain. I try to stuff my guts back around the blackened branch to which I'm mated. My fingers are warm for the first time today. If only I could stop my legs from twitching the pain might not be so bad.

The train is taking the turn in a languorous arc. It's a passenger train. There is a child aboard who is ill with something terrible. I cry. I can't help it. Her pain is like an absolution.

Figure 6: Digital painting, Lorina Stephens

The Gift

Without Laura's environmental data the geological report meant little. Again Brian glanced at the calendar on the computer. A dark square outlined today. To the right of that dark square was another day, this one outlined in red, red for urgency, and red because tomorrow was Christmas.

He shifted his attention back to the notes in front of him on the battered desk. All the words blurred. He felt the silence crush him. Laura should have been standing behind him, fresh from another analysis of Ela that garnered nothing. His wife would have praised his findings as if he had placed this wealth of minerals here in the Mackenzie Basin himself. Her hands would have been on his shoulders, her warmth palpable on his back. She would have said something like: "Brenley, come see how clever your father is," and Brenley would have careened over, excitement vibrating through her small body. Such a harsh place to raise such a delicate child.

He turned to where Laura should have been, reaching out for her, her dark hair, her slender body, ready to hold her and let her ease the rawness.

Brian found only Ela.

"What are you doing here?" he asked, his voice rough from disuse. It seemed bizarre to him that he spoke to a figment of Laura's insanity.

Ela frowned, that pale, elongated face expressing confusion. Everything about this woman wounded him: the way she watched, the way she spoke. She opened her mouth, but he pre-empted her.

"I know, I know. You don't understand what I'm talking about."

"I do not understand," she said. That voice so fluid, so aloof, as if he were a specimen she studied. He wondered if the Aleuts weren't right, that there were forces here in the Mackenzie Basin with which no one should tamper. Certainly Laura had said as much.

"Why are you here?" he asked.

"You were thinking of me."

"Bullshit." Her statement unnerved him. Around the image of Laura had been this mystery phantom she'd discovered and could never prove. When he asked Laura for data she'd shrug in a helpless gesture and mumble something about being unable to remember her data when with Ela. It had been like watching her drift away, marooned on a floe in the pack-ice. When she'd found Ela, the woman was just there, kneeling where Laura knelt examining purple saxifrage. Laura said Ela hadn't been dressed for the weather, but when queried as to how she had been dressed Laura had been vague; when pressed, answered, "I don't know."

How could she not have known? Laura was an environmental scientist! It was part of her training to observe.

And yet all the details about Ela were the same – vague. No data where the woman came from. No data about her background. Ela always just seemed to show up.

Now he shared Laura's insanity. He could find no psychological, chemical or biological reason why he did. Anyway, it mattered little he was going insane. There was no one to stay together for.

Don't go there. Don't think about that. To think about that was to let that howling thing in him climb up his throat, out his mouth and shatter everything he clung to.

"Why is it so frightening to you that you've accepted my existence?"

He wanted to shout: *Because you're not real!* Instead, he turned to his notes and the reality of one of the world's largest oil deposits. This was his chance to retire. No more scrabbling under adverse conditions. There would be a warm clime for him, a warm house. There would be people to grow old with. People to die with.

The thing in him gibbered up his throat, filled his mouth. He clenched his teeth, blinking the blur from his eyes. *No. You can't do this. You can't let go.*

"I am part of your reality," Ela said.

You are part of my insanity. How could he tell his insanity to go away?

"You are very special, Brian. Like Laura and Brenley."

"Don't talk about them!" He cradled his head in his hands, leaning against the desk. "Go away." *I have to finish this report. I have to get out of here.* Even if the supply plane wasn't due until a month after Christmas. "I have work to do." *Please, let me work. Let me forget for one moment that Laura and Brenley aren't going to walk through the cabin door.*

"What is this work?"

What was the point? He couldn't evade her. This was probably his way of linking to Laura and Brenley. "I have to find oil."

"Why?"

"Because we need to have it."

"How can you accept the existence of something you can't see when you can't accept me?"

"You're my madness. You won't be a problem for others."

"I could be."

He whirled on her, gripping the violence in his hands until his knuckles ached. "All I know is that my reality's twisted. You're not real, Ela. Nothing about you is real."

She smiled, all softness and compassion, so at odds with the aloofness she usually exhibited. As he watched her she seemed to glow. An aberration of Arctic light, he assumed, part of his growing madness or part of his grief. They were one and the same.

She spoke, softly, weaving the beginnings of a story, pulling at everything he locked into a safe place. The grief in him threatened freedom. Ela spoke of a woman, her hair dark, her body slender, a woman he had known, and loved, and been loved by, and as she spoke out of her aura stepped that woman, smiling, reaching out to him. Laura. So like Laura. Even her fragrance was there, clean, soapy, filling his senses when she wrapped her arms around him. Her lips parted as she leaned into him. He stood abruptly and threw himself onto the bed on the other side of the cabin, burying his head under the pillows.

How could she do that? How could she make the characters she spoke of real? But then Ela wasn't real, was she? Why shouldn't a thing from his insanity create people who weren't supposed to be alive?

He punched the pillows aside and glared at her.

"I don't understand why you are angry," she said. He ignored her comment, refusing to accept anything his mind created. She knelt before him, almost catlike. "I want to understand. If I can understand you then maybe I can help you understand me."

"Why should I even speak to you?"

"Because it would help both of us."

"You're not even real."

"What is real?" She reached up and touched the photo of Laura and Brenley that hung on the wall over the desk, cautiously, her long fingers testing the surface as if measuring just how far she could go.

"I miss them," he said, giving up, giving in, giving her the key to undo him.

She only stared at him.

But, then, he was only admitting his loss to himself, wasn't he?

༄༅

The Gift

To sleep would have been wise. To sleep would have let him sink into a place where memory and reality merged, where he was happy and Christmas wouldn't be a bleak promise. He'd been chasing sleep for hours now. To no avail. It was one of those nights Laura haunted him, Brenley in her arms, both of them lying like broken dolls dressed in clownish parkas, smashed in the rubble of a shale slide. He could still hear her telling him about her last encounter with Ela, about her frustration. His last thought before that roar had been one of despair, of Laura lost in a world of insanity. Then the earth had taken everything. His despair. Laura. Brenley.

He should have known. The shale scree was unstable. It was no place for his wife and daughter to be hiking. A geologist, fine. But not Laura and Brenley. He should have known.

He turned in the darkness and clutched Laura's pillow. The bed stretched around him, vast, empty, too much for one man to fill. He spread himself across its surface, trying to find Laura there, Laura's warmth, Laura's smell.

A movement on the bed stopped him. Alarm chattered down his limbs. Had someone sat down? He tried to hold his breath, to silence the rush of blood in his ears.

Light filled the cabin, radiant like candlelight. All he could think to do was clutch the pillow, his heart thudding painfully. It was a woman on his bed, slender, dark hair, that small mouth that could utter such brilliance in her field and such tenderness when it came to him. Her skin glowed softly. Lamplight, he told himself, knowing in that other part of him skin didn't emanate light like that. What was more, Laura was dead.

She smiled. "What would you like for Christmas?"

He tried to speak, failed, cleared his throat and managed, "You," convinced he had completely fallen over the edge. When the supply plane arrived the crew would find a drooling lunatic.

But it was Christmas Eve. Miracles could happen. That cold part of him laughed. Miracles didn't happen in the real world. *Get a grip. You're a scientist. You're suffering from grief and isolation.*

Laura laughed, like a caress. He shuddered. It was pleasant, insane though it was, to hear her laugh.

Oh god she seemed so real! And he wanted to hold her. Just for a little while. If this was insanity he would accept it. The bed was too large. His life was too empty. This place he called home was too sterile. He closed his arms around Laura, his mouth on hers. It didn't matter that he made love to a memory. It didn't matter that the woman he touched was no more substantial than the creature who visited him day after day since Laura and Brenley died. None of it mattered. Laura felt real.

This was Christmas Eve and he was making love to his wife, tasting her skin, touching her curves, whispering desperately indecent things as they moved in a way that was both selfish and selfless.

She shuddered against him, a cry in the room. He sank into a euphoria that seemed timeless and then ended too quickly. Sweaty, satiated, he rolled over and held her in his arms, stroking her hair, an emotion in his chest he couldn't name and was afraid to confront. It took two to fill this bed. That was as far as he would allow his thoughts to go. It didn't do to question miracles. Or the gifts of insanity. He didn't want to remember her broken under the weight of the slide.

"I love you, Brian," she whispered. And then his arms were empty, the light snuffed. That raw thing in him escaped. He sobbed into the pillow still damp from Laura's head.

⁂

In the end he must have slept, he realized, because he woke to that dim light called day in the Arctic winter. It was something he sensed rather than visualized because his eyes were sealed shut with crust. He rubbed at them painfully. Finally he looked around the cabin, to the dresser and small mirror on the wall at the foot of the bed, to the bed stand to his right. It didn't feel safe to look any farther.

He swung his legs over the bed. There was a chill to the floor. He wiggled his toes, careful not to let his thoughts begin, not to question, not to do anything to stir the dream and the nightmare of last night.

From somewhere in the back of his mind came a memory of the smell of roasting turkey, filling the cabin. His pulse lurched. He closed his eyes, willing this not to be. He could smell that turkey. It was stuffed with a sage dressing. His mouth watered. And now he could smell cider rich with cinnamon, cloves and orange peel simmering over a burner.

His hands trembled between his knees. He clasped them over his face. It was then that he was aware of the rise of humidity and the thick, sweet smell of plum pudding on the steam.

"Please," he whispered, unsure from whom he begged mercy, unsure even if he wanted to be delivered of his insanity.

There was laughter then, high and clear, that unmistakable giggle of a little girl. As if in a dream he hauled on his trousers, stood and paced into the centre of the cabin, sure of what he was about to confront, unsure of what to do about it. Against all odds there was a luxuriant balsam in the sitting area, its primitive, pristine scent impossible and marvellous. Trees like that didn't grow here. Brenley stood beneath its six feet, wrapped in a pink robe, her dark hair gleaming. She was so much like a miniature of her mother. She tossed silver icicles onto the branches, giggling when they caught, giggling when they fell. At her fuzzy slippered feet was an array of packages.

"Well hello, sleepy," Laura said.

Bewildered, he turned to the kitchen area where Laura stood fussing with crepes and applesauce and sausages – a traditional Christmas morning breakfast she dubbed French Piggies. That the ingredients for this dish were impossible to have at the moment didn't occur to him. It was the impossibility of Laura and Brenley that baffled him.

"Your dad's awake, Brenley."

Brenley turned from the tree, her dark eyes wide, her mouth an O of astonishment. She dumped the icicles and rushed into his arms. He opened them, mechanically, lifted her up and up, etching every line of this child he'd made onto his memory, relishing the feel of her small body against his skin. It occurred to him that it was these small things that made memories. A touch. A smell. A taste.

Had he remade her last night? Was that what he'd done when he'd made love to a ghost?

Laura was no ghost this morning. She set breakfast on the table and walked over to him, pecked him on the cheek, wrapped her arms around both him and Brenley.

"Merry Christmas, sweetheart," she whispered in his ear.

He could only nod, warmth rippling down his neck.

"Ela's going to have Christmas with us. Do you mind?"

He shook his head and let her lead him to the table where Ela now sat, another aberration of his mind suddenly there and real. They ate. He handled utensils without notice, lifting food that tasted wonderful to his mouth. He chewed. He watched these three females. They laughed. Brenley twitched with the prospect of presents. Ela said little. She just sat there glowing in that way she had.

Laura leaned toward him and wrapped her hand around his. "I think we better leave breakfast for now. Brenley's bursting."

His gaze shifted to his daughter, over to Ela and then back to Laura. "You're not real."

Laura smiled, squeezed his hand, looking at him the way she did when he needed her, when he was unsure. "Life isn't about happy endings, Brian. Happiness is what you experience along the way to death."

He yanked his hand away from her. "But you are death!"

She looked over to Ela. He stood abruptly. He was distantly aware of the chair overturning and clattering behind him. "I have to finish my report."

"It's done," Ela said. "There is no oil. Your resignation is tendered. You never have to leave."

He backed away, tripped over the chair, swearing when pain shot up his leg.

"Reality is what you want it to be," Ela said in that infuriatingly cool way she had. "You want your wife and daughter to be real." She shrugged. "They are."

"I don't want you to be real!"

"That's a reality I can't alter because I know myself to be real." Her look softened. "Brian, I need you to accept my reality."

"What are you really?"

"I'm what you want me to be."

What did he want her to be? A ghost? An alien? One of the spirits from Inuit legend? *Or do I want her to be my insanity?* "And them?" he asked, nodding to Laura and Brenley.

"As I said before, reality depends on perspective."

A life for a life.

He crossed to a chair and sank into it, watching his wife and daughter, the way they laughed, inhaling the smell of them, luxuriating in the reality of them. It was Christmas. Who was he to question the existence of miracles? Or to shatter them.

With a sob he slid off the chair and sat cross-legged beside his wife and daughter, ripping a bow off the present in Brenley's small hands.

Figure 7: Digital painting, Lorina Stephens

Over-exposed

Published previously, Maple Syrup Simmering, Fall 1995

He runs now, the siren hurting his ears. His legs rise and fall, rise and fall, although he feels as though he travels nowhere. Heat spurts through his chest. Adrenaline. His hand touches the camera bag. He looks over his shoulder to Kay and Meagan. His wife's face is red from running. She clutches Meagan's small hand. He tightens his grip on Chris'. In his mind the frame freezes – an image of terror.

Keep the children close.

He looks now to the escalator. It's crowded with shoppers who shove, fall, trying to escape to the shelter on a sub-level of the mall. The river of people becomes a torrent on the escalator as they tumble one over the other.

"The stairs, Peter!" his wife yells.

He veers to the left. His camera bag tags a display case. Royal Doulton explodes through the case to the marble floor. Still the siren shouts.

Get to safety. Get below. Get to where the terrorists can't get you.

A side-entrance to the mall flashes by. He changes direction sharply, grabbing Kay's hand. She loses her hold on Meagan. His daughter screams.

Kay scoops her up. He wants to clutch both children. He knows better. One adult to one child. That has always been their rule. It has always served them – against charging rhinos, in capsizing canoes, the fact that they took care of one child each brought them through.

He has to believe it will bring them through now.

The escalator in the empty hall is near. It remains motionless. He leaps onto it and bounds down, Kay close behind. A voice announces over the broadcast system: *Proceed to shelter.*

Another part of him notes the stilted cadence of the voice. Auto-systems are in place, he thinks, and sets off at a sprint when he reaches the bottom of the stairs, pulling along his son. His camera bag bangs heavily against his side. It does not occur to him to throw it away. So much of his life is tied up in that bag. He has run with it before.

Further down the hall the crowd pushes in from another entrance. Their screams mix with the siren.

"Hang on," he yells at Kay.

His wife clutches the strap of his bag and runs with him, his gear keeping them together. They break upon the flow of bodies, now pushing across them, sweeping down the hall in a relentless flow. He must reach the other wall. On the other wall is the door to the shelter.

Fighting, he comes to the centre of the flow. He cannot help memorize the faces around him: an adolescent girl, her face twisted with fear, black streaks on her face from mascara. He thinks of a battered harlequin.

He blinks and pushes further.

An old man, his eyes closed, carried like a grey leaf.

Almost to the wall now.

Fear is real around him. It is in the sweat of every body he shoves past.

Was it a dirty bomb that hit? Are there bio-agents hidden in that bomb?

He feels Chris' fingers slip. He grabs his son's wrist, tightly. Chris yelps. No time to apologize. His son's skin is damp beneath his palm.

He hits the wall and shoves his shoulder to it, moving in the tide to the door. It is within view. He can still feel a pull on his camera bag. Kay and Meagan are with him.

The door rises, slowly, inexorably, as if the floor sprouts this massive, white slab.

He lurches forward, shoving people out of his way. A toddler screams before him, terrified in the crowd. For a moment he hesitates.

The door is up half way.

His eyes still see that child when he shoves past. It has to be either his children or someone else's.

People stand before the ascending door, screaming, pounding on the concrete. Red splotches pattern the whiteness. People attempt to scramble over the top.

It is three feet from the ceiling.

He drags his family the final distance. The door rises still. He manages to hoist Chris to the lip of the door, yells at him to jump. He glances at Kay who is doing the same with Meagan. Chris disappears down the other side. Peter leaps. Two feet left in the opening. His fingers catch. People pull on his legs from below, trying to bring him down so they can come up. Concrete grazes his arm. In the moment he falls to safety he glimpses his wife and daughter falling away from him, back down into the mob.

The siren screams and screams in his ears.

These bombs go off in clusters now. They have become clever, these terrorists.

The door seals with a deep rumble.

Oh, God, Kay. I love you.

He presses against the door, his chest pounding. He is unsure whether the pain in his chest is fear or loss and realizes it doesn't matter. Chris is at his side, quaking. Peter slides down the door and gathers his son into his arms, tucks the boy's head under chin. In a moment he feels his son sobbing.

"What about Mum and Meagan?"

The pain in Peter's chest explodes. He has no answers. He weeps when the ground tilts beneath him; he clutches his son to himself. The sounds of grief keen through the shelter.

There are so many of them here - men, women, children, huddled together like lumps in a web. Their faces are distorted. Some scream. Some weep. Some try simply to organize in an attempt at normality. Some begin to strip and stuff their garments into plastic bags from the shelter's supplies.

Reduce the risk of radiation. Reduce the risk of contagion. Mechanically he forces himself and Chris to do as the others.

He closes his eyes to shut out the faces his mind won't stop recording. In the darkness there are only the faces of his lost wife and daughter.

Mercifully, grief exhausts him. He crawls to a corner and braces himself, tucking his son under his arm, his camera bag a pillow. It isn't the first time he's used it for a pillow.

There is a distant sound - the people in the shelter silence for it — thin, wailing, like the screams of all the world. It is the wind that comes after the blast. He knows if he can hear it they aren't safe. That becomes apparent when a hairline crack snakes down the wall. It runs from the ceiling to the frame of the massive door.

This, he also shuts out. For a few hours he and his son will sleep. Perhaps carbon dioxide won't fill the shelter. His mind flashes photographs of his wife and daughter, like a relentless slide carousel.

He wakes all at once. Chris stirs in his arms. He touches his son's yellow hair. It is damp with sweat. For a moment Chris looks up at him. His eyes are odd. Fear swells.

Carefully, he eases away, checking his watch. He has slept twelve hours, enough time for one of the designer viral hemorrhagic viruses to manifest.

He glances around. There are so many people here, bundled into blankets, whispering in groups, wandering idly. He rises to gather information. The survival of his son and himself relies upon that. Yet even as he passes through this, the main room, he knows there is nothing of survival here. Already sickness seeps among them. One infant is dying. He can tell just by the way it wails, frail and helpless. Other children are apparently dehydrating, swinging through fits of stupor and hyper-excitement. The smell of ammonia hangs in the air.

From here he walks down a wide corridor off which many rooms and dormitories open. They are all as crowded as the entrance where Chris sleeps.

When he passes one doorway the smell of food stops him. A man stands over a Coleman stove, stirring something in a black skillet. Whatever it is, there is garlic in it – savoury, unusually home-like in this grim place. A woman sits at a table nearby, cradling a girl's head on her shoulder. The girl's eyes are glassy. Like Chris'

He steps into the kitchen and sees another twenty tables around which adults and children sit. It is then he smells the coffee – burnt, acrid.

He cannot stop recording the faces. As if to find a focus he walks to the woman and the girl. The man at the stove brings the pan to the table and sets it down, offering the woman a fork. As Peter draws near, the woman tries to feed the girl yellow eggs. The girl, her hair a meadow of tufts, whimpers and turns her face to the woman's neck. A hopeless look passes between the man and woman.

They notice him now.

"She ill?" Peter asks. It is a stupid question, he realizes.

"She has cancer," the man answers. "We were taking her shopping before her next treatment."

His attention centres on the girl. She can be no more than ten. The lantern lights are harsh. His vision distorts so that there is only light and shadow. He thinks of the Sabatier effect, solarisation of film. She sits there motionless, all darkness and brightness, as if she were the print over-exposed to create art. Her hair forms the Mackie lines around her face – sharp scratches of whiteness where light meets dark.

With this light and a 100mm lens he could shoot at f8 for a normal exposure. But if he opened up to f4 that would over-expose by two stops, just enough to start the Sabatier on film. Just the way he had shot Meagan and Kay last year. The print won him acclaim in his last exhibition.

He blinks and the Mackie lines dissolve. There is only a girl sick with radiation. It is not cancer that kills her, he knows.

"She has cancer," the mother weeps. "It's the cancer."

It's not. He turns away to Chris, back through the corridor thick with people, back through the conversations of organizing, back through the people sleeping wherever they find a place.

His son still sleeps on the concrete where he left him, pallid, his head on the cushion of his arm. There are bruises on his son's arms – ruptured cells, haemorrhaging. He knows when Chris wakes hyper-excitement will set in, his nervous system under attack. There will probably be seizures like epilepsy. He's read about some of these new viruses. Science designed for destruction.

Carefully, he slides down the wall beside his son. He hides his weeping behind his hands, his shoulders shaking. How is he to save his son from this?

After a while Chris awakens and complains of hunger and the need for a bathroom. Peter nods and composes himself. He leads his son through the shelter to the bathrooms. From there they go to the kitchen and find a meal being served. They sit. They eat.

He watches the girl who has cancer. She is still lethargic, resting her head on her arms.

His attention flicks back to Chris. The boy shovels canned stew into his mouth, oblivious to the chatter around him.

A man shouts over the noise, bringing the room to silence. The organization of survivors begins. There has been no radio contact. They have no idea if rescue is coming. A doctor is identified, then a biologist. Other people with their own fields of expertise come forward. Labourers, office workers. Peter stays silent. They will have no need of photographers. It wouldn't do any good anyway. He doesn't believe in digital photography. All his film is exposed, he knows. Use a dirty bomb to deliver a double threat.

The meeting goes on for hours. There are arguments over plans of action. He becomes aware of Chris sleeping against his arm. Carefully, he carries his son back to their corner. Chris sleeps while he remembers those last moments when he lost Kay and Meagan.

He wakes to the sound of people calling breakfast. Now there is a queue for food. Oatmeal.

He takes coffee and makes sure Chris eats. They find a table and sit.

The girl with cancer fidgets this morning, dark smudges like charcoal under her eyes. Her mother leans toward her, whispers. The girl bursts into tears and flees the room.

At lunch he catches only a glimpse of her as she darts in for a peanut butter sandwich and darts out.

When dinner is served she doesn't appear at all. He can hear her, though, racing through the shelter, screaming. Her mother sits at the table and weeps, her husband's arms enfolding her.

That night, after the lights darken, Peter's attention is drawn by a flurry of sounds near the kitchen. He rises, walks, his steps quicker as he sees lights. When he enters the kitchen the girl thrashes on the floor in a seizure. The doctor is with her, trying to free her tongue. Too late. She bites it. She screams and screams. Her mother sobs in great shudders, clasping her hands to her face. A foul smell rises from the girl as she loses control of her bowels.

"It's the cancer," the mother mumbles.

The doctor stares at her bleakly, returns his attention to his dying patient. The blood won't stop coming.

Peter turns away, his hands impotent, and makes his way through the sleepers to his son. He eases down the wall. With his fingers he traces a line along his son's cheek. He presses his lips against that cool skin, straightens.

He flips open the bag filled with two cameras, film, lenses, flashes. The Nikon is in his hands. It is a battered camera, all manual, better artistic control that way. The 100mm lens is on. His favorite. A lifetime of creation in this camera.

He fingers the black strap, his attention sliding to his son who sleeps fitfully. The strap is still strong, even after al these years of use.

He inhales sharply and slips the strap around Chris' neck and pulls. His vision of his son blurs, as if he were shooting a frame with a Vaseline screen. Chris kicks, his hands tight around his father's arms. Peter tries not to look, his eyes hot with tears, his skin crawling with horror.

He still weeps when he goes back to the kitchen for a chair, brings it to where Chris lies, climbs it, hooks the camera over a support beam, ties a knot that will tighten with weight, and slips his head into the strap. No one pays attention when he kicks the chair out.

Figure 8: Digital painting, Lorina Stephens

Zero Mile

While the others slept, Ayrin Johnson stared at the bands of light on the ceiling, stripes of white and black, a geometry created by the lights shining beyond the closed blinds of the room. He should have been sleeping. That would have been wise. Tomorrow would demand his most excellent performance.

A ripple of movement snared his attention. Not in this room. No, it was beyond, out in the hall. His handler. He could see Bob just as clearly as if he were standing before him. But Bob wasn't. His handler paced the hall purposefully, his gaze intent upon the door of Ayrin's room, his hand reaching for the security lock, palm sliding across the plate.

Ayrin's eyes took over. Bob was no more than a shadow in the rectangle of light at the door, a motion of a hand beckoning to Ayrin. Come.

Pep talk. Ayrin could sense it in Bob's energy, the way the heat bands shimmered and shifted around Bob's body. He swung his legs off the cot and rose, crossing to the door in two strides. The light of the hall filled him. He turned his face up to the glowing ceiling.

This was sheer pleasure – to feed upon this light.

"Are you okay?" Bob asked.

Ayrin's turned his gaze down to the man. Of course he was okay. Wasn't that obvious?

"I could put you in a different room for tonight."

A room of light? Sure. Bob would do that. Anything for his prize runner.

"I know you'll do fine tomorrow."

At least you hope I will.

"I can understand why you lagged so far behind the others in the qualifying heats."

Of course you can. Bob had told him often enough not to let the other runners know just how fast he could cross distance. Speed like Ayrin's was to be guarded.

His handler reached for Ayrin's arm, withdrew, warned by the immense heat of the runner's body.

And the Angels Sang

"Your times tomorrow have to be good," Bob said after a moment.

What was good? Hadn't Roger Bannister's four minute mile been good? Noah Ngeny's 3.32.07 1500 metre? Dayo Ibibio's 2.55.32? For that matter, hadn't all those shaven times pleased these people? Was it necessary to cross the distance of space in a few short seconds?

"Three seconds just won't cut it."

Not with these people. They were so impatient. It had taken Ayrin's kind millions of years to evolve to this state.

And yet these people were so close. They knew now that astral-projection was more than hyperactive imagination. Proof that people could leave their bodies behind and perform tangible acts elsewhere had been in existence on Earth for some time now. All they had left to learn was to take their body along with them. The mind was an infinite thing, capable of feats only the aboriginal peoples could imagine.

And Ayrin. He could imagine. There had been the wonder of it before the crash, of people so at peace with themselves and their surroundings that nothing was impossible. Any reality could be created if only you *believed*. It was something the Earth Messiah had said. It was something the Buddhists cloistered in mountain retreats knew. And now with the Unification Theory so close to being proved shifting through time and space would soon be a tangible reality for them.

He looked back over to Bob, the pain of memory like a wound within him. If only he could retrieve that time, the time before the crash when he'd been with his own kind.

Bob smiled. It had nothing to do with humour. It had everything to do with frustration. "Look, if you don't do well they're going to want cell samples."

For cloning. Ayrin denied them that. He'd have no part of their research. There were already too many freaks running this race.

"This is important, damn you!"

Ayrin just stared.

"Won't you talk to me? Ever?"

What for? Communication wouldn't be achieved.

"It's been ten years, Ayrin! Don't think I don't know you can communicate. I've caught you at your telekinetic play more than once. God knows what else you can do."

Ayrin turned away for the door.

"Just once, Ayrin! Talk to me!"

The palm-lock released. The door swung open. Ayrin stepped through.

He could hear Bob swear as the door sighed shut.

Perhaps he should have offered his handler some comfort. But what? What could he possibly give him except a new record?

His turned his attention to his roommates, motionless in their sleep, each cocooned into a bed of their own. Perhaps it was fitting he would run for Canada with freaks like these. A freak with other freaks. He was one of them.

Ayrin folded himself into his cot, unable to stop his inspection of his companions.

Rikker in the bed next to him was something he wasn't entirely sure was human – two-thirds legs, one third cardio-vascular system, and pumped full of oxygenated blood and nutrients by an extra-body pack. Speed was the reason for Rikker's existence, and Ayrin wondered if he weren't as hideous. What was the difference, really, between experimental body modification and evolution?

He closed his eyes, soaking up what little light the blinds afforded. Hideous or not, he would win the race tomorrow, and win it so that the title will be forever his. His reasons had nothing to do with wanting to please his handler.

When morning finally came he'd been up for several hours, drinking in the dawn. Bob had accosted him once more. That conversation had been as futile as last night's. They always were.

Now Ayrin stood at the starting line, his feet tight against the blocks, his muscles, tendons, mind screeching for a win at the fifteen hundred meter finish. He searched in anticipation of the starting blast.

Memory overwhelmed him. He remembered another blast, all of it orange, red, orange-gold, like a sun being born and burning him with brilliance. There had been voices in the blast, screaming with whining metal that gyrated like massive shrapnel. Often he'd wondered if those bits of bodies – an eye attached to a nose, a fragment of lip, third joint of an index – had streamed in glorious plumes of colour with the metal shards, or if they'd charred and slopped soggily to the snow. Even now the horror of it seemed unreal.

Had there been spirals of steam?

And why had he lived?

The cheers of the crowd shattered his thoughts. He glanced up at the carbonate wall around the track, at the thousands crammed into the amphitheatre. A red and white flag snagged his attention. They were waving it for him and the other Canadian runner.

His gaze settled upon his competitors.

Eight other bodies strained in an arc that splayed out behind him. They fretted, fidgeting to find the right pressure against the blocks. A groan rose

And the Angels Sang

from one. Another whirled and kicked the block. Ayrin bent, doing nothing, feeling nothing except a cool knowledge he would win this race, and win it without contest.

He coiled into his position.

The runner next to him made some lewd remark about Ayrin's legs. Ayrin offered no reply.

"Hey, Arctic runner – too frozen to talk?"

Ayrin kept his gaze to the fore. The other runner abandoned his taunts. Ayrin knew that would happen. He'd learned early that time was his companion, and so cultivated a past-time of shock-my-guardians. It hadn't taken him long to realize he was different, and that difference would keep alive. String theory manifest. Even at the age of six when he'd been found near the wreckage the scientists had been very clear about that. Freaks, especially freaks that could run, received luxuries. And lived.

But why had he lived?

Again the question seized him, as it often did when he stalked those seconds before the race. He felt himself harden like the rock of an inuksuk, out of place with the riotous emotion of the moment. He waited.

The other Canadian runner answered a gibe with, "I'm running for my country," as if Ayrin weren't running for the glory of country and conquest at all, as if he had nothing to do with this Olympics.

Ayrin let that one slide as well. There were a few talents he'd kept guarded from his well-meaning guardians. Even Bob hadn't a clue just how quickly he could fold distance.

He smiled. If only they knew. Even his unofficial time a year ago of a two second run had been enough to send physicists, paranormals and biologists reeling. Their amazement still puzzled him. They had been so in awe of him, so incapable of accepting proof of their theories.

Again he saw that exploding ship. Why had he, of eighteen people aboard that craft, lived? It was impossible, unfair, a twisted joke of fate that he should be an island in time, hopelessly marooned in a life that had no meaning but the running of the race and breaking the two second record. That, in itself, had no meaning. What could be accomplished, for them, by smashing time out of rational understanding? They didn't even comprehend time. Oh, they played with it in their theories of dimensional realities, measuring the universe for fluctuations of gravity.

But for him it was different. He'd broken through the membrane, slipped on a string. And now it was necessary to compress those membranes again. If he could defy the measurement of motion to time, he would answer why he'd lived.

That thought only reminded him of his isolation and alienation.

He shuttered his eyes, shuddering, for a moment losing his concentration. Another runner tossed him a covert glance, grinning, his skin tinged with blue from the speed-enhancing drugs to which he'd become addicted. Ayrin could *see* him despite his closed eyes, revolted by genetic engineering that created this creature.

Still the crowd cheered around him, the runners restless. It seemed to take so long for everything to coalesce.

He opened his eyes, scanning the walled track where the eyes of halo-cameras scanned him. The cameras were there for the protection of the runners. A good runner was under constant surveillance. As the fifteen hundred meter's time decreased, a runner's susceptibility to political subterfuge increased. The runner assassinations he'd seen sharpened his understanding of how serious this Olympic race could become.

Sweat sealed his skin in a slick, slimy film. A word formed in his throat, found shape on his tongue and before he could stop himself said it aloud - ship - and even then it was a hollow whisper caught on dry lips. The first whisper in ten years. The other runners ignored him, his break with silence too minute for them to notice. For Ayrin it was a word of hope. If he could *see* the ship before explosion, fix it firmly in his mind, it would act as a magnet for that moment he would slide sideways into faery, follow a string that connected the membranes of the universe's time and dimensions. Achieve that, and he'd witness what went wrong.

It occurred to him it was now he who fretted, just as had his fretting rescuers, fretting guardians, fretting trainers.

A signal passed from the judges in the carbonate cube to the linesman. Ayrin watched the man intently. He could feel the linesman's finger twitching over the siren's touchpad. Excitement sliced through him. He squashed the emotion.

One of the runners leapt out of the blocks and was into the second hundred metres before officials managed to net him and bring him back. That would cost the runner; calorie consumption would slam into a hyper-burn. If the race didn't fire up soon, the runner would collapse.

Even as he thought that he could feel another part of his brain coil, tighten, strain, prepare for the massive leap his body would take through physical space.

Believe it to be so.

And then it started. Time liquefied around him, as if he rode the eye of the storm. Let it go. Do it well enough and he'd be there, paper folded through a tube of time. Astral-projection in the real sense. His muscles slackened while the other runners tensed. They seemed to spin, caught as time flowed through an endless gyre.

It happened. The stuff of black holes. How it was his people propelled their void-ships, searching through the gyre of time until they *saw* where they needed to be and then hurtled off like a planet thrown from the centrifuge.

The starting siren blasted.

The clocks hadn't begun to count the first milli-second when he folded matter and time into a tube. It was all about structure, you see. He felt himself stretching, singing with the tightness. Matter wavered and he was fluid in the centre, a strand of jelly threading through a dancing mass.

He realized then what the crash had meant, and again was joined with his family. Nothing for him had changed. He was home. It was like music.

She was there, his host, the female who sheltered him in her womb.

She smiled. The power of that gesture moved like motion through him. He smiled back. Joy giving joy. His gaze slipped to the navigator who was suspended in null-g, a man he called his maker, the mate of his host.

Too late Ayrin realized he'd reached for his maker with his thoughts.

No!

Cries rose around him. Maker cringed, his eyes wide and staring into a place Ayrin couldn't see.

"Don't!" his host screamed. "Ayrin, stop!"

Too late! Already the ship faltered, dangerous for their proximity to Earth's atmosphere. Ayrin reached through time to clear a path for himself. He was young. Inexperience sheared a shallow channel, space enough for only himself.

The ship flamed a bloody tail. He could only watch the carnage. The vortex of time folded in upon itself. His body snapped into the future stream. The other runners sprang from their blocks.

The horror of that moment hung with him. He swallowed, only to find his tongue glued to the roof of his mouth. But there was hope. He knew now where his ship had been before the disaster. Reduce the race to zero again and again, and again he could be with his own, maybe one *time* enough that he could fix his consciousness into that stream. And then he realized one other fact – the race gave him purpose.

Already he stood beyond the other runners, at the finish line. His breathing was even, steady, a smile that felt like triumph on his face. The sound of the siren still echoed in his ears. The sounds of the *others* still lingered, lapping over the roar of the shattered air. The time pieces ticked into point zero one seconds. A cacophony of voices rattled the carbonate cube, drawing up his gaze. One judge's face was utterly burlesque as it pressed again the clear surface of the booth, mashing the nose into something resembling a squashed banana. He laughed. The sound of it was wondrous.

It would take another two minutes for the holos to be verified. That didn't bother him. This race was the only way he could discover the truth about himself and why he lived. The results would read a Zero Mile.

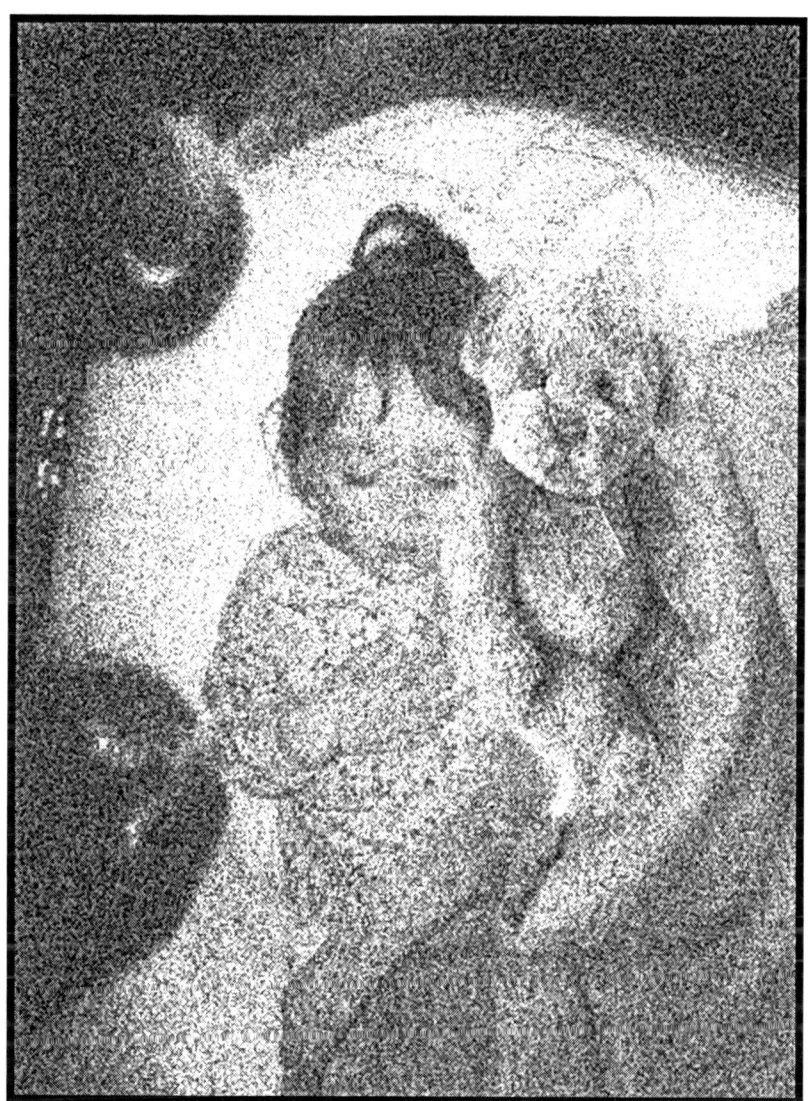

Figure 9: Digital painting, Lorina Stephens

Darkies

Melina lay sweating in her bed, the thin, cotton sheet clutched to her neck. Dusk gathered at her window. Around her lay an army of friends: Panda the Bear, Trixie the Dog, Greenie the Teddy. A stir of air rustled the plastic drapes, false promise of relief. She longed to lay back the sheet, neatly, without disturbing dust that would have her wheezing inside of moments, but that would mean lying exposed in her room and she had learned the better of that decision. Safer to lie sweating with the sheet as armour and the peaceful purple of twilight to rock her.

The purple at her window was like the purple of her walls, clean, dreamy. She sang a song about that, silently, because it wouldn't do to make noise and draw attention. Besides, there were some things too special to say out loud.

> *The purple grows outside my window.*
> *The purple grows inside my room.*
> *Darkness coming in the garden.*
> *Darkness coming in my room.*
> *The Darkies, the Darkies, soon they will come.*

Oh, yes, the Darkies. Two nights ago she discovered them in the four corners of her room. Two nights before that there was only one, and that a shadow of a man.

Uncle Julius, small and dark, like a monkey she thought, with that scary look to his eyes like the monkeys in the zoo who watched you and knew, they *knew*. He had the name of kings, an emperor, so Mama told her in her casual, careless way. Melina wondered if all kings dealt so sneakily, so cruelly. He had been just a shadow in the corner of her room long after the purple faded from her window and the world was wrapped in darkness and shadow, blacks and blacks with only the silver and grey of moonlight when it shone through the glass.

And the Angels Sang

She had been singing - well, humming - quietly so as not to bring down Mama's anger. Mama didn't like noise or bother or disturbance. The song was one Melina made up for the beauty of the night. When the shadow in the corner of the room had separated from the walls and took on the form of Uncle Julius, she stopped singing, that last note silenced in a moment of fear.

The monkey was loose. And he knew; he *knew* things that would make her be silent. To her bed he crept, like the bogie-man himself, dark and silent. In her head she sang:

> *The purple grows outside my window.*
> *The purple grows inside my room.*
> *Darkness coming in the garden.*
> *Darkness coming in my room.*

Then he was there beside her bed, his hand on her mouth, in her face the smell of pee and sour toilets.

Melina didn't want to remember that and felt sweat trickle down her face and slide round the curve of her neck. She pulled the sheet closer still, making sure the edges were wrapped tightly under her arms.

> *The purple grows outside my window.*
> *The purple grows inside my room.*
> *Darkness coming in the garden.*
> *Darkness coming in my room.*
> *The Darkies, the Darkies, soon they will come.*

In her head she heard them come, long, slender people-shapes that were neither man nor woman, all blackness and shadow. Darkness dripped from their long fingers, flowed from their long hair and grew like grapevines across her walls.

We are here, they sang, all whispers like breathy angels.

> *We are here. Sing, Melina, sing, for we are here and darkness grows,*
> *Outside the window, in your room, darkness coming in the garden,*
> *Darkness coming in your room.*
> *We are here, and none will fear,*
> *While we watch and you will croon.*

Relief flooded through her and for a moment she dared to let go her grip of the sheet, sit up and bow to each of them, elegant creatures. They bowed in return, like dark water rippling. She sank back down to the bed, the foam pillow, and held the sheet back to her throat. For a while she would be safe. They would watch. They would sing with her. And tonight, tonight, maybe when Uncle Julius came she would find the courage to sing out loud and end her torment.

For a time they sang the Song of Darkness, silently, all of it weaving like heavenly music through her head. They sang low, like a slow moving river, like the wind in autumn. She could almost smell these things rich and healthy unlike her and her sickly lungs. For her part they let her take the high notes, and this she did gladly, in her mind letting her voice slide like a wheeling bird high and higher, rising and rising to the moon.

She was almost there when another shadow joined them. Her singing stopped. The Darkies' did not. She still heard them like the earth itself, rocking, comforting.

None shall harm thee,
Child of the night, and child of the morning.
None shall harm thee but that thou sing
Sing, sing and be free!

Her throat tightened and she tried to breathe, felt her chest freeze and her lungs betray her. It was as though Uncle Julius put his knee on her chest from where he stood in the doorway, suffocating her. He moved, gracelessly, through the doorway and quietly closed the door, turned and continued to the side of her bed.

As always he said nothing, hobbling like a beast. His hand closed over her mouth. She could see nothing of his face, turned as it was away from the window. He was all shadow and beast-strength, smelling of sweat and food. She knew what would happen next, shrank at the though of it. She tried to be small, so small she would disappear under his hand, that her mouth would not be large enough to do what he wished.

In her head the Darkies sang:

None shall harm thee
Child of the night, and child of the morning.
None shall harm thee but that thou sing
Sing, sing and be free!

Free, oh, Mother Mary, yes, she thought, let them be free, please Mother, let them be free; and all at once she felt her song in her head, felt the notes travel there in their sweet, sad purple sound, rising and rising. She opened her mouth. She heard Uncle Julius sigh with pleasure. Song spilled out of her, thready and hoarse, but song nonetheless.

The purple grows outside my window
The purple grows inside my room.
Darkness coming in the garden.
Darkness coming in my room.
The Darkies, the Darkies, soon they will come.

Uncle Julius retreated a step, she thought surprised at her song. She sang the song again, trying to find enough breath to finish. Out of the corners she could see darkness flowing, detaching from the walls. It moved like cloth through the air, fluid and comforting, and then tore apart like scarves to wrap Uncle Julius softly, all the while their music like rapture in her head:

We are here!
Sing, Melina, sing!
For we are here and darkness grows
Outside the window in your room
Darkness coming in the garden
Darkness coming in your room.
We are here!
And none will fear while we watch and you will croon.

She heard Uncle Julius gasp. By now the Darkies lost all form and were no more than flowing scarves around his body, his thrashing limbs. He did not cry out, and she was glad of that because she was afraid to make any noise but for her singing which was soft so as not to make Mama angry by disturbing her world. She dared to sing higher, higher yet, her lungs cooperating and giving her breath, while the Darkies' song lowered and slowed like the wind in autumn, like the chattering of dry leaves. Soon Uncle Julius was all but invisible inside that swirl of darkness. She sang her last, trembling notes as the scarves faded and melted away.

There was grey now in her room, promise of dawn. The Darkies were leaving, in shreds and tatters, gathering into the folds of her plastic curtains, the drapery of her sheets. Of Uncle Julius there was no sign.

She looked to the window and saw the paling sky, remembered the hymn they were practicing in choir:

Morning has broken, like the first dawning.
Blackbird has spoken, like the first bird.

Darkies

Praise for the singing.
Praise for the morning.
God's recreation of the new day.

Drawing her knees to her chest, bowing her head upon her arms, she sang this, silently, because there were some things too precious to sing out loud.

Figure 10: Brush & ink painting, Lorina Stephens

A Case of Time

Petra didn't hear her companion's screams, couldn't see the way her face twisted into a parody of death. It was all she could do to breathe, to keep her senses centred on one thing at a time. At the moment it was upon a shape on the floor. How many lives ago was that?

No matter.

What did matter was that it looked odd - that shape on the floor - odd in a way that made her tremble. She didn't want to look at it. Papa demanded that she look.

From where had Papa come? She was having an argument with Sabine. Papa was ....

Petra knew not to look would mean more of her blood would add to the pattern. It was something her body remembered, and something of which her body warned her.

She remembered reaching with her fingers for the corner of her mouth - then, not now - felt them slide into the stickiness there. Such pain. She inhaled the pain, letting it keep her sane. If she could just focus her gaze on that blot, so like a butterfly, Papa would go away, leave her to contemplate the repercussions of defying his wishes. Just this once, Petra thought, she might escape form his demands. Futile. She remembered him grunting over her like some panting dog, and now she had this pattern on her bedroom floor to remind her that she was his possession.

Fear stilled her pulse. This was a memory she shouldn't have. It was supposed to be banished, incised from her life like a discarded limb. That was supposed to be what the Relocation Process did. Remove memories. Harmful memories. Memories that might seal her into a life of constant repetition.

But the memory was there. As real as her breath. The bloody butterfly, she remembered, had filled her eyes until sundown when Papa returned. When he touched her shoulder - she knew that touch - she made his body create a pattern of its own. A dead pattern. A dead body.

"Stop! Please! Petra!"

That hoarse cry was present. Vaguely she was aware of that, but somehow it seemed unimportant. She knew she had to run.

She *was* running. In her mind she remembered running, running into the roaring heartbeat of the spaceport where she lived.

It hadn't been hard for her to find sanctuary in a stairwell. She'd folded herself into that gloomy triangle, shivering. A pair of black shoes rose and fell across the floor. She closed her eyes. She'd forgotten about police, about the fact they might find her father. Her body, she remembered, trembled so violently that her stomach knotted, heaved. She swallowed. Bile ran bitterly along her tongue. Quiet. She must remain quiet and then creep toward a freighter on which she could escape. It was all just a case of time.

Time. That was past. A forbidden memory.

Now she heard her companion's screams – immediate, yanking her back from that place of memories. The screams faded like echoes lost in the void of space. Petra's gaze came down. There was a face at the ends of her hands, a face twisted into a mask of terror, exaggerated, the way a mime might exaggerate.

Why have I done this?

The thought shattered the dream-quality of the moment. Her hands sprang open, as if she were afraid of touching the dead thing that had been Sabine. Sabine who used to fill her with excitement. Sabine who listened to all her secret memories, and later, when familiarity was nothing but contempt, twisted them into agonizing weapons.

Sabine's body fell like a doll to the floor, creating a pattern of its own. Was it always to be like this? Love corrupted? A bloody butterfly?

The door behind her breathed open, a uniform in the rectangle. The man's gaze was hard. Petra said nothing to defend herself.

What was there to say? That the sight of blood on her coveralls reminded her of a battered butterfly? That seeing it was more than she could bear? That somehow she knew this was a memory she shouldn't possess?

He wouldn't understand. She wasn't even sure she did.

The next hours slid by like cinema. Being jailed was familiar. It shouldn't have been. Arraignment was familiar. Neither should that have been. She had the feeling all of it had happened before, that she'd never managed to escape from the sight of her father's dead body, stolen passage on a freighter, that she'd stood before this court, then, perhaps even many times before then.

Reality lurched. Nothing stood still before her eyes. She could only see bloody butterflies. Everything else had that taste of repetition, as if she were condemned to perform this same sequence of events over and over and endlessly over.

A Case of Time

She was aware now of being in a courtroom, a room that was non-descript grey, a small cubicle in which only she was a physical reality. The holograph of the judge, sacrosanct in her black gown, asked her if she was aware of the Relocation Process. She nodded. She shivered. The judge inhibited her, overwhelmed her in a way she found new, different. How should she react to this demigod? Even in holograph the judge's authority immobilized her. All she could think was – *this is a judge, Angel of Justice, giver of life and death.* This was the same power as her father. The feeling was completely different.

Petra longed to fold herself within her jumpsuit, crease her body into a tiny packet that could slip away on an errant breeze. The judge's voice startled her out of wishes.

"You understand what will happen in this trial?"

Petra nodded. How could she not know? Everyone knew what happened when brought before the court. And yet Petra's knowledge sprang from taboo.

"Explain," said the judge.

Petra forced life into her tongue, moved it, placed sound into her mouth for her tongue to form: "Time will be folded so I can go back to the crime. Judge and jury witness."

The judge nodded. "And if you're found acceptable, we'll place you into the Relocation Process."

That statement fell through Petra like ice.

The Relocation Process.

Infamous! A new body. A new identity. A new location. Would she remember anything of her present life? There *were* memories she longed to possess, those few stolen memories of contentment.

"Must I go now?" Petra asked.

The judge dipped her head in a nod.

So powerful that movement. Not even a word spoken.

The holograph faded. Petra knew the illusion of isolation was just that. Somewhere beyond this grey room the court assembled. The dais on which she stood would condemn or condone her actions.

Petra frowned.

Had she done this before? Had she stood on a dais like this, felt the weight of the court, swung back and forth through time like a pendulum caught in perpetual motion? Had she?

Sweat chilled the envelope of air between her skin and her shirt. She was sure there was a dark stain on her back.

Had she done this before?

And the Angels Sang

She glanced around the room. Walls, floors, dais – all grey. She knew that. She shivered. Why was it so cold? Again she narrowed her attention on her surroundings, trying to identify something, anything in this sterile room.

Why was she here? She found no memory to appease that question. Memory seemed to have evaporated with the holograph. Her head tingled.

The sweat on her back chilled, cold, even colder. Ice. Ice between her shoulder blades like a knife slipping, sliding between the vertebrae of her spine.

Why was she here?

She shivered convulsively now, her jaw chattering so intensely she was afraid of chewing her mouth. There was a salty taste there – salt and copper, fear and blood.

She blinked. There was a voice ... two ... now several ....

They were watching!

Those unseen, all-knowing people behind the voices. They sighed and whispered like forgotten wind in forgotten trees. She whirled, desperate to put faces to those voices. Nothing.

Her shivering eased, stilled by that cold thing in her spine. Was it real? Had somebody put something into her spine?

She blinked again. A room she knew settled around her, a womb of reality. The voices seemed less important now. What did they matter? This room was real, vaguely familiar.

Hesitantly she stepped from the doorway into the room, her feet feeling thin carpet, rough, like crackers under her toes. It didn't feel right. None of this felt right.

Had she done this before?

Surely she had. How many times had she walked through this door, into this room of a home, every line of her strained from a shift with the ore-diggers?

Her gaze jerked up, still filled with the colour of the carpet, blue she remembered, and swept the single room of her home – a communication screen, refrigerator-heating unit set into one wall, a beige plastic protuberance which served as a table. Stools – two of them – sprouted like mushrooms on either side of the table. Not far from this two junk antique things were set at right angles to each other in the centre of the room, facing the com-screen. The chair was Petra's. The floral divan was Sabine's, her companion.

Something helpless, hopeless hurt her. She couldn't name it, but its source was in this room. She *knew* this. It was like a shout in the furnishings, the air, the carpet still like blue crackers under her toes.

Her stomach lurched. That sickening sense of vertigo threatened her again, that feeling she'd done all this before. Her gaze shifted, hung upon the door. Something dangerous would happen when the next person came through that door. There would be words, angry words that left bruises and pain. She was so sure of it. Even now, standing there, she could hear the sound of those words, feel emotion shove her past the threshold of restraint.

Her gaze fell to her hands – clenching, unclenching, almost like lungs filling and collapsing. She raised her hands palm up, stared at them, turned them and let them drop back to her sides. A seat would be good. Stand any longer and her knees would liquefy.

Petra slumped into the derelict chair. The relief she found there was short-lived. Her companion flounced into the room, brazen in films and furs, paint like a mask. Tension crawled in the room with her, the memory of an ongoing argument still there in Petra's head. There had been such pain associated with Sabine, such betrayal. She now remembered endless months of it, bitter words, sleeping alone only to awaken later warmed by Sabine's body, the smell of someone else lingering between the sheets, on Sabine.

At first she simply turned away from the hurt, letting the pillow suffocate the pain. Later, when Sabine's name was the brunt of bawdy jokes in the mining community, Petra found it difficult to smother that seething thing inside her.

Now she could do nothing but glare. This taunt was too open, too much like a threat. Her companion hadn't even bothered to disguise her infidelity. It was plain from the way she dressed she'd been prowling.

Sabine, you whore! Slut of a tramp I should have divorced before now!

It was the same anger, the same hurt she felt with her father.

Her father? At that moment she knew she wasn't supposed to remember her father. That was a memory alleged to have been silenced.

But why should it have been silenced? She couldn't answer. She only knew the knowledge was dangerous, illegal.

Petra guarded her knowledge and her words, letting her glare wither the smile on Sabine's face. Only for a moment. Hardness congealed Sabine's features. This was a reaction Petra knew. Sabine delighted in that subtle form of torture. Sabine, as always, remained defiant, taunting. Even the way she curled into the divan hit Petra. This would be one of those silent evenings that seethed with tension, a cold war.

Petra fidgeted like an insect, desperate to keep the thing inside her caged. A word to the com-screen caused a swarm of holos from the only vid-station. It was a sit-com designed to appease Luna's working class and it did everything to appease Petra for a moment. She even found herself laughing at the antique comedy.

Sabine, on the divan, laughed also. Petra's sense of déjà-vu crashed around her. Her laughter froze. A face of terror.

Had she done this before?

Are you sure everything's the same? someone said

Petra pressed her fingers to her ears. From where had that voice come? Her gaze swung over to Sabine. Her companion only laughed, that gusty laughter that had at one time been so inviting and now only taunted. It was only a memory. A memory of something precious and lost.

Petra inhaled, desperate to calm herself. Perfume, Sabine's, heavy and flagrant, assaulted her. Her senses clouded. Her eyes watered. Pain like a drum-roll thundered beneath her skull, threatening to split open her mind

"Do you have to walk around the station like that?" she said before she could censor her tongue.

Sabine parried and struck. "Yes. I have to. It's the only way I know I'm real. You certainly don't acknowledge me."

"How could I?" Petra stiffened against the lumpy chair. "You've enough paint on you to cover an entire freighter."

It's the same, said another voice.

Had she done this before?

Sabine uncoiled from the divan.

Petra flinched. The grin on Sabine's face reminded her of the way her father grinned – fangs. Sabine had her cornered, one hand clamped to each arm of the chair. Instinctively Petra's gaze shot to the shadow and swell of Sabine's breasts ... right there ... in front of her face. Even as she did that, she knew Sabine still smiled that vicious smile. Petra longed to rip it off her face, the way she had longed to rip the smile off her father's face.

I think history will repeat itself, a new voice said.

Anger writhed in her like a clutch of snakes. She wanted to match venom with venom. As if it weren't hers, Petra's hand surged into the air and detonated on Sabine's face, creating a crack and breeze as her companion's head reeled and Petra's fingers, palm, wrist sailed by

Her palm and fingers coagulated into a fist. The momentum of her anger carried her fist back, her eyes full of nothing but the sight of bloody butterflies. The sound of splintering bone was vaguely familiar to her. From somewhere else she stared at the grotesque angle of Sabine's jaw, the way a crimson ribbon fluttered from the corner of her mouth and dripped, drop by coppery-smelling drop to Petra's grey coveralls. The blotches of blood formed a pattern in her lap. She thought of bloody butterflies. It brought memories of its own, memories unformed but there, lurking, like forbidden fruit.

I'm not so sure, someone replied to the earlier statement. *Perhaps history won't repeat itself.*

With a cry like a charging beast Petra vaulted out of the chair, clamping her fingers around Sabine's throat. Her companion's eyes bulged in disbelief.

For Petra there was only this sensation of familiarity, that she would forever feel flesh under her thumbs, rubbery, flaccid, that adrenaline would give her the strength to do what she had been unable for so long, enough so that she panted, sweated, her heart palpitating. Petra found herself echoing the sound.

It's the criminal element, someone, somewhere else said. *Either you are or you aren't. I knew she would be.*

That was when Petra stopped shaking her. That voice had referred to the *she* as Petra.

"I'm not!" she cried, releasing Sabine as if her fingers had been burned. Didn't they realize a person could tolerate only so much? To prove a person innocent by taking them back in time to the event was fine, but what followed a judgement of innocence was a hell of its own, a hell of shadows. A new body and a new location weren't enough. She had no sense of continuity, of belonging. How could she without some tangible, permanent memory of what went before, landmarks to guide her? How could she be sure that she hadn't endlessly murdered, received pardon and a new life?

Her gaze shot back to Sabine. "Get out! I'll file for divorce in the morning. By evening you'll be free. Get out!"

She lurched off Sabine. The sense of déjà-vu fled.

"Get out!" she said again, watching Sabine scurry to the door and freedom.

Petra's knees liquefied, her body falling although she felt as if her mind remained caught somewhere else while she slid, slipped, wind screaming across her body like ice.

The wind stopped. She continued her descent and crashed to the floor. A floor without carpet, a grey metal floor that was warm. Brilliance as hard as diamonds scratched her eyes.

The courtroom.

"She's innocent," someone said, really said. "She's proved that it was a crime of passion, and in the same historical circumstances avoided repeating the crime. The jury suggests relocation to remove any negative influences."

She raised her gaze from the dais and stared at the holo of the judge stone-faced and bored at the bench.

"You're found innocent by this court," the judge said. "All charges against you are dismissed. The Relocation Officer will take you for treatment to begin your new existence."

New existence.

So it was to be a new life, high-tech reincarnation. Just how many lives could she have? And would there always be bloody butterflies at the end of every life?

Figure 11: Digital painting, Lorina Stephens

Jaguar

It was brief, that howl, but enough to make her slam her back against the wall, shove her palms to her ears. She slid to the floor, trembling, chewing on the horror of what she'd done.

"Erdoes," she breathed, shutting her eyes to the sight of her kiln. "I had to. Please understand I had to."

The howl died. So did Erdoes.

Jadis buried her face into her knees and tried to smother the memory of his agony.

Two days later the kiln cooled enough to open. The clay sculpture proved powerful, a splendid interpretation of terror, futility, all of it screaming from the tense lines which ran to the gaping oval of his mouth, the hand outstretched for sweet refuge that didn't come.

"Lift this to Abram's gallery," she barked at the com, turning her back on the howling man. Why should this commission be any different than the others?

It didn't occur to her the answer lay in her clenched hands.

❧|❧

Two weeks did little to appease her growing malcontent so that by the time her show opening arrived she was in no mood for chatter.

But there would be chatter. It was the way of all exhibitions. Abram, her agent, passed her to the Panasian Ambassador.

"Jadis, darling, the world will think you're brilliant because of this show."

She raised an eyebrow to that, kept her attention on the sculpture before her of the clay man. It occurred to her this was probably her best work. In both careers. What would Ambassador Kuo do if he knew how this particular piece had been created?

"I didn't think the world would be interested," she answered. She knew the timbre of her voice would affect the small Panasian. It was always a good tool. And it did. He shivered, stepping nearer.

"Not interested? Why – "

"Perhaps Jadis is uninterested in what the world thinks," someone else said, his voice mellifluous, menacing.

She flicked her attention to the man who now stood beside her – the triangular frame that tapered to thin hips, the long legs. As always his face was the last place for her eyes to rest, and the effect was, as always, the same. A shiver ran down her spine, something somewhere between hot and cold, pleasure and pain. She couldn't think of a time she hadn't thought of Amaru as a snake – tan and black, sleek, long, deadly. A bushmaster. He was that, a venomous viper. She should know. She'd been spreading his venom for several years.

She didn't spend a welcome on him. It was almost a ritual between them. He leaned toward her, nuzzled her cheek. Ice. She afforded him a minute smile. She turned her attention back to Ambassador Kuo.

"You will excuse us."

The Ambassador bowed away.

"I understand this piece is under reserve bid," Amaru said, nodding to the sculpture.

Of course it was. He knew that. It abraded, this game he played.

Her answer was tacit, her gaze flicking to the passers-by, the other pieces she'd created. They drew comment, attention, but none the speculation this piece garnered.

"It makes an excellent complement for the rest of the series," Amaru said.

Again she nodded.

"By the way, did you hear Commissioner Erdoes is missing? They think he disappeared into the Green Zone."

Erdoes! "Pity," was all she answered.

He patted her hand. His skin was golden, almost iridescent against the darkness of hers. "You're the best, Jadis. But you don't need to hear that from me."

She removed her hand. "Payment is still made with the cashier."

His wide mouth curled into a smile. It was hard. She could almost feel herself chiselling it out of golden marble. He bent, bowing, elegant. She took a long breath when he turned toward the cashier.

Why did she let him affect her like this?

The sculpture drew her attention away. Even now she could feel the dampness of clay under her fingertips, as she had when she'd moulded that ruddy earth around a human form. It had been the seventh in a series, all commissioned and purchased by Amaru, all hits he hired her to perform. This has been the most difficult. This hit had been her lover, a lover not by choice but by design and later choice came into her life. Erdoes had been so noble, so pathetically noble in his attempt to squash Amaru's poaching of fresh water. But what good did it do? People like Amaru breathed power, incarnated power. What did noble ideas have against that?

And her relationship with Erdoes had been business. It was something she reminded herself often. She'd been hired to dispense with this annoyance to Amaru and so after three months of intimacy she sedated Erdoes day after day, entombed him in clay and fired him in her kiln. His assassination should have been no different from the other officials'. It was. It was different. This she couldn't deny.

She looked back to Amaru. A card passed from his hand to the cashier's. He didn't even bother to verify what had been transferred. Jadis knew he wouldn't. He left. Silent. Without fanfare. It was always this way with him.

A scream ran through her head – Erdoes. Why had he screamed when the others had been silent?

A desert replaced her mouth. She reached for the first glass on a floating tray, tossed the champagne into the back of her throat and replaced it before it was an arm's length away. The champagne did nothing to stop the scream in her head.

"You okay?" Abram asked, drawing near.

She nodded.

His hand pressed her arm. "You're sure?"

She nodded, flashed a superb smile from her kit of theatrics and engaged the next inquiring patron.

Throughout the evening she did that – smiled, nodded, reacted like a well-rehearsed mannequin while her mind analyzed the past years of her life.

What would she do if not what she did? To sculpt, yes, she would always sculpt. But what of the assassin? Was that person weakening? Was that why Erdoes still screamed in her head?

That question occurred to her when the last guest left, several thousand credits lighter.

"Superb!" Abram crowed.

Jadis flicked her attention to Abram, sweet Abram who was always there to listen, to encourage, to stoke her fire when she had nothing left. He paced toward her, his pudgy arms wide, face aglow with admiration for her. When he folded her into his fleshy embrace she thought she could stay there, never think of living the life she led.

It would end, this comfort. And it did. Abram held her at arm's length, the sweetness of his cologne intoxicating.

"You are a marvel, Jadis. Sold out again."

She shrugged a smile.

"What? Not happy?"

"Ecstatic."

His arms fell away. "I'd hate to see melancholy."

Her gaze turned back to the central sculpture, the piece Amaru purchased. "Just tired."

"More than tired." He nodded to the howling man. "Amaru purchased the clay."

"I know."

"He has them all."

She made no reply.

"What is it, Jadis?"

"What's what?"

"You – what's up with you?"

"Should there be something wrong?"

"You tell me."

Why not tell him? Abram would understand, he always did.... "Do you ever..." Her gaze came back to him. "It's been a long night."

He frowned, turning her toward the lift. "It *has* been a long night. Get some rest." He paused when she stepped into the grey cylinder. "Consider a sabbatical. God knows you can afford it."

In the next moment she stood in the lift of her home, an order on her lips to keep the lights low.

A sabbatical.

It had the sound of paradise to it – tempting, luxurious were it not for the serpent. Would Amaru even consider freeing her from his employ? With what she knew?

Sleep, when it came, was bereft of refuge. She dreamed of Erdoes, the hell he'd endured in those brief seconds of consciousness. She dreamed of a viper that encased her in clay.

The next morning, while cleaning her kiln, the terror of the night persisted. She could settle to nothing, flitting from work to coffee to work. She slid her palm along the floor of the kiln. For a moment she stared at the fine white dust on her hand, talcum-like. This had been Erdoes, his only crime to stand in the way of a demand for fresh water ... and fall in love with her.

A chill fell down her spine. The controls chimed, announcing a delivery. She barked to have it sent up.

Why react like this now? Wasn't she seasoned, a professional, beyond this kind of bleeding-heart paranoia?

She stepped out of the kiln, wiping her hand over her shirt, leaving a white slash on her dark smock. A box sat in the grey cylinder of the lift. She knew who had sent it and what it contained. A chill took her again.

White trilliums, the ends dark where they had been singed. They lay in the box like fragile clouds, petals colourless as sleep. There were more here than she'd ever received, evidence of Amaru's gratitude. They were expensive, contraband, part of the forbidden Green Zone. He always sent her white trilliums at the completion of a contract. Dinner always followed.

She traced one of the tissuey blooms with her finger. Two dozen of these plants were now dead, all to satisfy Amaru's need. She could almost feel Erdoes shaking his head in sorrow. He would have called this gift obscene. Perhaps he was right.

Should she have dinner with Amaru or escape? It was possible to escape, to disappear. Her clandestine career gave her access to a number of means. She could simply have a body-change, slip into another city-dome and start work as a new person. What about leaving altogether? Leap forward in time? Or the Green Zone?

It was possible. She had access.

The com warbled.

"Who is it?" she snapped.

"Amaru," the unit answered.

Take his call? Her gaze descended to the trilliums in her arms. Why not?

"Put him through."

"Are you rested?" he asked.

She flinched. He was always overly concerned with her health, as if she were in imminent danger.

"Quite."

"I'm glad." She bet he was. "I thought we'd have a small celebration here tonight."

"At The Nest?" In her mind she could see the opulent villa floating above the towers of the city.

"I thought it would make a nice change."

Alarms rang through her. Amaru of all people loathed change.

"I'm not bedding you."

Laughter. His laughter was always so silken, smooth, sinister. "I didn't ask. I just thought dinner here would be calming for you. After all, it was a late night for you, I'm sure."

To go? To The Nest? She shuddered. But she'd not reveal her apprehension to him. That would be a mistake.

"Whatever suits you," she answered.

"Eight, then – our usual time."

Usual time. Different place. Experience told her something was wrong.

"Of course. Shall I dress?"

Laughter again. "You said you'd not bed me."

"Don't' be vulgar."

"Yes. Dress. Something gold would show off your skin nicely."

The com warbled, a signal to the end of the communication.

So this was to be a showing off. To whom? To all the empire Amaru wielded?

She dumped the trilliums into a tank of clay, suddenly sickened by the gift.

"Coordinate visual on the Niagara Escarpment and north of Gitche Gummi." It would be a good idea to see the areas Amaru pillaged. How was it that she had researched all of her hits so well, and researched so little about the man who hired her? Surely she hadn't been that blinded by his power, his wealth, his silken way of dealing with people?

"Where would you like to see the file?" the com asked.

"In the bath."

Why not sit in water while studying water? Best to be well-informed before seeing Amaru this evening. She had the feeling she stood at a pivotal place. It even affected her decision to accept his offer. Should she go? Or not? Would he hunt her if she abstained? If she went, what had he planned? Surely something. Dinner was to be at The Nest.

Another hit? Would the hit be her?

Damn him.

No. Damn her. She was the one who had let down her guard, enchanted by this bushmaster. She should have known better. It was prudent to remain alone, in isolation, always stalking her world from the fringes. She had failed to do that with Amaru.

The bath, when ran, was hot, fragrant with the scents of pine and wildflowers, scents that threatened to dissolve her icy armour. Erdoes had often smelled like this, especially when she'd meet him after one of his expeditions. She had almost gone with him into the wild, silent forest of the Green Zone. Almost. Truth was when Erdoes spoke of the forests, the springs, the lakes, his passion frightened her. How could he have loved something that couldn't speak? Something that couldn't return in kind? She'd asked him that. He'd answered with a question: How could she love her sculpture?

Jadis sank to her chin in the bath and let its narcotic spin through her head.

"Run file."

The com silently complied.

For the next hour and a half she travelled the length of an escarpment that thrust like a giant's rib from green, dark forests. Springs, a meromictic lake among others, rivers – all pulsed through the ancient sea wall. Water in rock. Rock to support tree. The infinite blue sky a veil of protection.

From there the land gave way to Gitche Gummi, a lake the size of a sea that still garnered legends. Erdoes had spoken of those legends. A manitou who had returned once the Green Zone was established and again beat a rhythm for the cycle of life. Here granite rose in sheer cliffs, twisted into faces that haunted the clear, cold water.

Beyond this was a forest of lakes, a place the Anishnabeg walked for 10,000 years without mark. It had taken the Europeans only 600 years to violate that sacred pact.

"Overlay 500 years prior," she said, straightening from the cooling water, her knees in the circle of her arms. She inhaled sharply when the holo came up. What the com displayed was a scene far more drastic than she had anticipated.

"Indicate which water systems have dried naturally."

One percent. That was it. The remaining fifty-three percent drained before the establishment of the Green Zone.

And was still under attack. She could think of it no other way.

And she had helped. She may not have drained water herself, but by performing the hits Amaru asked of her she was as guilty. All those hits had been people involved in the protection of the Green Zone.

"You have to care," Erdoes had accused.

The only thing about which she'd cared had been her sculptures.

"Display off," she said, sheeting water as she rose.

Water.

From hidden tanks in her studio. A gift from Amaru. The condenser/purifier remained inactive. How long had it been since she'd rationed water?

"Activate water systems."

What was this? A sudden case of guilt?

She hurled the towel at her reflection in the mirror. Tall woman, ebony skin, pale hair that tumbled down her back and over her muscled body. Her eyes were blue, like the colour of Gitche Gummi. She remembered Erdoes saying as much.

Her head swam, her mouth bitter with bile. She reached out for support, and the moment passed as quickly as it came.

She stepped from the tub into her dressing room. The com warbled when she slid into a gown Amaru had requested of her, a gown that formed a cowl at her neck, concealed her arms and swept at her ankles. It *was* gold. It did nothing to show of the colour of her skin. It did everything to emphasize the blue of her eyes, the paleness of her hair. All things considered she was an exotic sight, she decided.

The comb warbled again. It was Abram.

What could he possibly want? She had him put through.

"This piece is excellent, Jadis!"

She frowned. "What piece?"

"The wood you just lifted down."

"I didn't lift anything down." To the com: "Holo this." Abram, or at least Abram's holo, appeared in the room, beside him a modest sculpture in pine, a woman dipping her hand into a pool. "This isn't mine." And yet ....

The lines of it flowed the way she would have made them, creating counter-rhythms between natural grain and artist's interpretation. But this piece surpassed anything she'd attempted, as if this artist knew her methods and refined them, honed them to this sparkling, sharp edge.

Her gaze flicked to Abram. He frowned.

"Stop playing," he said. "You've marked it."

"Where?"

He turned the piece, pointing to the base. She had the holo enlarged.

Her mark. She couldn't dispute it. But she hadn't created this piece. She wished she had.

"It's not mine."

The holo returned to normal view.

"You're sure?"

"I tell you I didn't sculpt this."

"Are you saying it's a forgery?"

"Did you get a trace on the lift?"

"Of course not. Why would I?"

"I think you should."

Audio blanked while Abram acquired the trace, then: "Stop playing with me, Jadis."

"I'm not playing games."

"Then explain why this piece came from your lift."

The hunter in her tensed. "Lift it back here."

He smiled nervously. "Then you admit you're playing games."

"Just lift it back here."

She had the communication cut, not before she heard Abram say, "Christ, Jadis –"

The sculpture materialized in her lift. She reached for it, her fingers trembling, and withdrew.

What was this pounding in her breast? Afraid? She?

"Put this on a pedestal."

The com did so.

A woman bending to water. This was not the kind of work she executed. Still, it had her touch to it.

Who would do this?

Amaru? But for what purpose?

She exhaled, steadying herself.

To set her on edge. That was purpose enough.

"Get me Abram." She waited the moment it took, and then: "It's me. Will you be around later this evening?"

"How much later?"

"Late."

A pause.

"Look, Abram, I need to talk to you, but not now, not here. Can I call you?"

"Are you in some kind of trouble? Is that what that piece meant?"

"Later. Say I can come see you later."

"I'm always here, Jadis. You know that."

She said her goodbyes, and lifted to Amaru's. Into The Nest. Hands formed fists, relaxed, fisted again. She realized what she was doing and forced herself to ease. It did nothing for the tension inside. That was fine. Just keep this veneer intact.

Her gaze flicked over the foyer into which she materialized – pink granite, the real thing, a white pine bound to a stone pot reaching for the dome of light. One of the servoids greeted her – a male replicant, white, beautiful. It would have to be beautiful.

She gave the servoid her name, remained in the lift. Around her the security systems blinked through a check. They'd find no weapons on her. Jadis learned long ago a good assassin didn't carry weapons. They could only be turned against her.

"Ah yes," the servoid said. "I'm instructed to bring you cocktails on the north terrace. Your pleasure?"

"Nothing." She stepped from the lift. Amaru would be late. It always made for a better entrance.

Time alone on the terrace sounded like a good idea. Time to think.

Scents smothered her when she stepped out to the gardens, rising from the pseudo-flora that bordered the area. Had she not known better, she'd have thought these plant replicants real. Only the best for Amaru.

Her gaze spilled off to the left where there were no gardens, only the odd drifting cloud. She walked to that, leaned on the railing and gazed down into a bowl of lights like diamonds in a saucer.

Only the best. He would have it all.

"Jadis."

The 's' of the word hissed slightly. She kept her back to him, knowing she was vulnerable and yet knowing Amaru was also. This wasn't the first time she'd met a threat with her back exposed.

"Amaru," she answered. His name sounded like smoke in her mouth. She felt more than heard him move behind her.

His finger traced a line down her back. "You wore gold."

"Of course." She kept her gaze within the city lights below, wondering if Amaru reached down how many of these shiny things he could scoop away.

He turned her with both his hands, a smile twisting one corner of this mouth. "It doesn't show off your skin." His finger sketched her aureoles where they pulled at the fabric. "Such a pity." He flinched, glanced to where her nails dug into the thin material that stretched over his groin.

"Only certain of my services are for sale." She smiled. "But, of course, you know that."

His nostrils flared. She knew that danger signal. His fingers dropped from her breast. Her hand fell away from his groin.

"Just a little play, Jadis."

"I'm not your playground." She nodded to the open door. "There was a dinner invitation?"

"Of course there was." He waved her to enter and she did so, letting her senses shift to her back where he followed. Danger. It was there. It had a prickly sensation all of its own.

There were no other guests expected as was evident in the two place settings at the enormous agate table. Surprise after surprise.

She sat to his left, not before an exacting glance at her seat. There were things that could be hidden there. She'd done it often enough herself.

The sculpture of Erdoes stood across from the table in a crowd of six other clays, lighted from below which only exaggerated the terror in those faces. She blinked, turning her gaze to Amaru and let it stay there.

He made light conversation while dinner was served, each plate individually prepared. When he chewed his first mouthful she lifted her fork, toying with the salmon, aware they had not been served from one plate.

Amaru smiled. "You've been the assassin too long," and forked a mouthful of everything on her plate.

She returned his smile. Nothing mitigated the danger she was in. She knew that. The danger lay elsewhere, that was all, if not in the food, then in the utensils. Did he really think he could beat her in a game of assassins?

"I'm afraid I'm simply not hungry," she said, pushing the salmon apart. She noticed the slight change in the red hue of the flesh where the fork had touched, something most would never catch. The silverware was tainted with a chemical that would react with bodily fluids. Even as she thought that she lay her fork aside, reaching for the thin fabric on Amaru's arm and let her fingers caress him deeply. "Don't worry. Being an assassin keeps me alive." Not once did she drop her gaze. Only a twitch at the edges of his eyes confirmed her suspicions. 'Now, why don't you tell me why you wanted to celebrate at The Nest?"

"I've another commission for you."

Had that been triumph in his voice?

She withdrew her hand, knocking over the glass of water by her plate. As she planned, it tumbled toward her, dousing her contaminated skin. Apologies and a hasty mop up did nothing to abate Amaru's anger; that was as plain to her as his amateur attempts.

"I'm retiring," she said finally, tossing her napkin onto her plate. The dark stains from the poison were garish against the white linen.

"I think you should consider this one."

Here it came. "Why?"

"Because someone called Jaguar is not only causing my business to suffer, but is tracking you."

"That seems unlikely."

"Had it occurred to you there might be an assassin out there better than you?"

"That also seems unlikely."

"You shouldn't be so sure of yourself."

"C'mon, Amaru, we both know the other houses have tried to take me out, and they with power and influence. The best have come after me. They haven't succeeded. You're going to have to do better than that."

He rose from his chair and strode to the howling man, his back to her. "Someone known to us only as Jaguar is sabotaging our missions in the Green Zone. Equipment and crew go missing without trace. We just lose contact."

Too bad. "How do you know it's this Jaguar."

"Jaguar leaves a calling card." He turned toward her then, his eyes like shards of terra cotta. "Very arrogant."

"Well."

"A debit to my accounts for time lifting."

Time lifting? Forward in time? Backward?

"Under the name of Jaguar," he finished.

"I still don't see what you need me for. This Jaguar can be easily traced."

"This Jaguar manages to wipe records. All we know is that he, or she, lifts through time, but to where we haven't a clue. We only have the lifts Jaguar's accessed. Yours seems to be a favourite."

Her brow arched. "Mine?" She shook her head. "Not possible."

"You care for documentation?"

So he'd taken it that far. But her lift?

The mystery sculpture occurred to her then. Was she being stalked?

"How long has this been going on?"

"Nine months," he answered. "Just about the time you took on the last contract."

Erdoes. Her gaze swept over the clay, the howl rising inside her.

Not now. Not here.

"And just what exactly do you want me to do?" She almost bit her tongue but she had accepted the contract before she had time to veto herself.

"What you always do."

Kill. That was what she always did.

"My price has gone up."

"Of course it has." He smiled. Something in that smile alerted her.

"No deadline on this one," she added. "Time lifting is an exacting science."

"Of course." He motioned for her exit.

That was that.

She left for the lift feeling as if something had been forgotten. It wasn't until she arrived back in her home she realized Amaru hadn't asked for another clay. That omission was now an ominous thing.

A trap. She could smell it, an old, familiar smell. So many had tried to trap her, unaware of whom she was, only aware they were the prey.

This was something for which she'd prepared. She gave instructions to her com to print a file long ago saved, a file that would ensure the trap closed around Amaru when it closed around her. While that ran she changed into her working clothes, those of the assassin, not the sculptor.

All her affairs were organized by the time she contacted Abram, late as she'd expected.

"Can I still lift over?" she asked before he had an opportunity to say a word.

"Jadis?" he asked, his voice clogged with sleep.

"Can I still lift over?"

"Of course."

She cut the link and stepped into the grey cylinder of the lift, a thumbnail file in the zipper-tab at her throat. When she appeared in Abram's home he was there, waiting, cinching the tie of his robe. It was plain he was anxious.

She did nothing to allay that. She stepped from the lift, unhooked the black cowl that encased her hair and most of her face, shaking out her hair.

"I need to talk," she said.

Abram swallowed, trying to unglue his tongue. "Of course." He gestured to the door behind him.

She strode into the white room, folded herself onto the sofa and kept her gaze fixed on him.

"I'm taking a sabbatical."

He mimicked a smile. "That's wonderful - "

"I want you to keep an eye on my studio."

"Of course - "

She tossed the thumbnail toward him. He caught it and looked a question at her. "Everything you need to know is in there, instructions, what to do, what not to do - "

"You're in trouble."

"Yes."

He managed to keep his voice steady, for which she was grateful. "A lot of trouble."

"Yes."

"How long will you be gone?"

"I don't think I'm coming back."

Ah.

She watched him struggle with that, saw how clearly he wanted her to come back. She looked away, an uncustomary flush on her face. "Will you make love to me, Abram?"

He stammered, completely off-balance with all the inconsistencies she threw him. She knew she was being unfair.

"Please," she said, her gaze still in her lap. "I'd just like to share something special with you before I go, before you read what's on that file." Her gaze came back to him. She let her features soften. "Please."

He seemed to melt, set the packet aside, leaned toward her and let his mouth answer whatever things she found herself incapable of saying. His lovemaking was not passionate, nor physical, rather one prolonged voyage of tenderness, patience, so that when he brought her to pleasure she cried and curled herself into his shoulder.

The moment ended as it had begun, without preamble. One moment she allowed herself to be soft, vulnerable; the next she returned to the shadow-creature of her craft. Her last words to him were: "Review the data. Destroy it immediately after. Wipe the lift records pertaining to this visit."

And that was that.

She lifted to the Green Zone, a pack on her back, into the Bruce Peninsula where Amaru had an operation that tapped myriad springs. Her first priority was observation. This operation of Amaru's was familiar to her through what Erdoes had told her. The main camp was settled into a bowl around which the escarpment towered on three sides. For kilometres the operation extended through rock, feeding off water that flowed through the ancient sea wall.

It had been prudent for her to lift here this late at night. And very much a risk. The lifts were the hub of the camp as it was from here water was transported back into the city-domes and from here personnel were ferried.

As she expected, a guard was altered by the com. A calculated blow to the back of his neck took him down. He'd wake with a headache worse than any hangover. She slipped from the lift and slid into the shadows of the forest after making note of how many buildings there were, the guards, the type of armaments.

Fortune was with her in that it was a moonlit night and that made the treacherous journey along this outlier safer than it might have been. Here a ridge of rock had been separated from the main escarpment when ancient glaciers melted and boiled through a spillway, and in the process eroded the outlier so that it was pocked with caves. When vegetation again returned to the region, trees had taken hold in centuries of humus that collected in the rocks. What evolved was a treacherous web of roots through which she could fall at any moment.

Even with the moonlight her way was unclear. Dew glistened off leaves like a forest of eyes, shadows like holes, holes like shadows.

The accident happened without warning. One moment she was testing the ground. The next she slid, a scream clamped in her mouth. Somehow she managed to claw onto the fibrous edges of the hole, clinging to the ancient roots. Her legs dangled into void. Better not to look.

For muscle-tearing moments she hung there, swinging her feet to find something as a foothold. Nothing.

Weak for her efforts, she strained to pull herself out by her arms, hoping the roots were strong enough to hold her. And at last she was on her belly, the cushiony web beneath her, the all-important pack still secured to her back.

That night she continued on all fours.

By the time she managed to descend the ridge and scout the caves for a likely camp, the woods were grey with dawn. What was to become her home was a cave created by enormous boulders of the talus that had stacked together to form a cone with a shaft above. There were only two ways in or out. Through the top. Or through a narrow passage between the escarpment face and the talus.

That could work both for and against her. Just as insurance she spent the early morning constructing a series of traps and alarms so well-hidden as to be unidentifiable from the surrounding woods.

For the rest of her first day she slept.

Over the next three weeks she came to know the area personally, intimately, understanding why it was Erdoes fought so hard to preserve the Green Zone, this section of it in particular. His last howl was with her, a cry that vibrated through her until it became an anthem, a war-cry, a thing that drove her over the weeks. And changed her. Where the forest had been her enemy, it was now her lover, as intimate, tender and sacred as the moments she'd shared with Erdoes.

She hunted for food, sparingly, quietly, supplemented that with an abundant supply of roots and berries. All things considered she was comfortable except for those few occasions she'd experienced a profound sense of disorientation, as if she didn't fit into the moment. That was the only way she could think of it. Each time she was left nauseated, as if her balance had been set akimbo. She attributed it to her primitive lifestyle.

But never did she encounter the Jaguar.

Several lifts back to her studio had been made, each time to access information about Amaru and this illusive Jaguar who was said to stalk her. The last time she'd dumped everything into the palm-comp she carried with her. She found no evidence she was trailed. It wasn't until the end of the third week that a series of events gave her reason to suspect that something truly exceptional was going on.

As usual she'd documented exactly what occurred with this operation, just how much water they shipped, how many people manned this post. She was wrapped into the cool shadows of the pines, watching from her aerie atop the escarpment. A shipment – a collection of grey containers – was about to lift away in the enormous cylinder. The lift activated. The shipment paled as molecules were broken down into atoms, formed strings and bled away. And then it seemed to Jadis as if the whole think blinked. It wasn't more than a mille-second. But she saw it. It blinked.

Personnel sprinted toward the area, orders flying.

The shipment disappeared from the lift, as it should have, and yet there was definitely pandemonium down there.

Had there been a blink?

The answer became obvious when the Chief of Operations fired out a stream of invectives. She caught little of it. What she did catch was important.

The shipment hadn't arrived at its destination. Amaru would be furious. Millions had just been lost in the matter of seconds. Erdoes would have been ecstatic.

She lowered the field glasses.

Then where had it gone?

While bedlam blew through the camp, she slipped the micro-com from her pack and tapped at the touchpad. The signal was aimed at the com in Amaru's camp, in particular at the program that ran the lift. With a little luck, and a little speed, she'd be able to access the log before it was wiped, as surely as it would be wiped. That was one fact about which Amaru hadn't lied, as she'd come to discover on a few occasions.

The answer she received this time didn't make sense. This lift? The shipment had lifted to this lift?

She saved that material just as the record from the com below was wiped.

She sat up.

How could the shipment have disassembled and reassembled on this lift? It wasn't here.

She stuffed the micro-com into the pack and turned for her camp, suddenly uneasy. That disoriented sensation came over her again. Nausea gripped her. Her head felt detached and for a moment she wondered where she was. The moment passed.

She didn't assign the incident to inconsequence any longer. What just happened was important, she was sure.

What greeted her back at camp unnerved her even more. The deadfall was down. There was no victim. The pit had been breached. Nothing lay inside. Poison darts were released. No dead body sprawled on the ground. All of the traps had been sprung and yet nothing had been caught, as indeed something should have been caught. She was a master of her craft.

There was nothing left to do but circle round and scramble up the escarpment to where the upper hole of her cave would be apparent. When she finally managed to peer down the opening she nearly slipped from shock.

A fire had been lit, and her com was on. Even from here the holo was clear.

Anxious, she shrugged off her pack only to find the small square of her com gone.

She stared out into the silent forest.

But the com *had* been in her pack. She'd used it back at Amaru's camp.

Her gaze dropped back to the empty pack, fell down the hole to where the com glowed.

She remembered the mysterious sculpture that had been lifted to Abram's, her frequent feelings of disorientation and the recent occurrence at Amaru's camp.

"*All we know is that he, or she, lifts through time, but to where we haven't a clue. We only have the lifts Jaguar's accessed. Yours seems to be a favourite.*"

Amaru's statement did nothing but fill her with dread.

She rose slowly and clamoured down the escarpment to the cave, sinking to her haunches before the com. The message that hovered there was plain in its intent.

Crane Lake awaits

It was signed J.

J for Jaguar.

It could have been J for Jadis.

Her fingers trembled when she deactivated the com and stuffed it back into her pack. The buttery glow in the cave chilled when she kicked out the fire.

It could also mean Amaru toyed with her.

Crane Lake. She'd travelled there before, investigating the operation. It was a place that had an ambience she couldn't name; it haunted her, a still place where it seemed everything remained breathless, even down to the pumps that were draining the ancient body.

There was no choice but for her to return to Crane Lake, picking her way with care, sure to keep to the trees and cover of the rocks. The operation was closing down for the evening by the time she arrived. Such luxury Amaru afforded his people. But he *could* afford it. Key officials were his playthings, his access to the Green Zone assured, his rape concealed. She should know. She had been integral to that.

Again she heard Erdoes' howl.

Amaru was that sure of himself there wasn't even any security at this instalment.

She crouched in the trees as the last of them left.

"Hot bath for me," one of them said. Jadis could have touched the man's legs as he strode by.

"Why not?" his companion said. "We've enough water!"

And they laughed.

Jadis hardened with anger.

Another moment passed before she slipped out of cover. Everything here was veneered in blue shadow, dominated by the hills that loomed on two sides. To the east lay meadow that was showing signs of reforestation – birch shimmering gracefully in the red light of sunset, cedar growing densely where water puddled, and oddly enough, apple trees, descendants of some ancient orchard planted by some ancient Irish.

She stepped to the edge of the tiny lake. It would have been perfect were it not for the hoses curving like giant leaches into the water. A birch towered gracefully in contrast, its reflection like a pale ghost.

Without realizing what she did she unclipped the cowl and shook out her hair, bent and slid her fingers into the liquid jade before her, letting it dribble through her fingers. The reflection of herself fractured.

At that moment so did her reality.

That reflection!

She inhaled sharply and rose, her heart thudding like a tolling bell.

Her reflection had been of the mysterious wood Abram had received.

But how was it possible?

Her stomach knotted. Nausea again. Alarm needled her back and she whirled, searching the woods for her prey.

And there. Just a blink. A woman with skin as dark as sleep, pale hair, blue eyes, a sinuous creature who moved like fluid ... and was gone.

She cupped her palm over her mouth.

"We only have the lifts Jaguar's accessed. Yours seems to be a favourite."

Her lift. Someone who would be wily enough to outfox her.

It was then she asked herself: Had Amaru hired her to hunt herself?

The need for her to return to her home was urgent and undeniable. For the second time in her life terror ruled her actions and she ran, a shadow in the trees, desperate to hurl herself into the lift in the main camp and flee from the Green Zone.

She reached the camp at a full run. It wasn't subtle but it had shock effect. She was within two strides of the lift before someone managed to gain enough presence of mind to fire at her. The shot didn't hit true. Laser-fire caught her in the calf. She pitched forward, biting a cry. Pain threatened to take her senses, but she managed to roll into the lift just as light criss-crossed around her.

A man yelled, "Get that bitch!"

Her fist slammed into the control panel. "Toronto," she managed to pant. "1000 Burfield. Suite 8201."

She watched a direct hit bloom before her eyes when the lift dissolved her into atoms.

The next thing she heard was, "Don't come out."

Pain seared her vision but she managed to squint at her surroundings. It was her home. Of that she was sure. And she was also sure she stared at herself. Not a reflection. Not a holo. Herself.

And the Angels Sang

Nausea got the better of her this time and she heaved to the side of the lift. That did everything to amplify her agony. When she wiped her mouth she caught the stranger doing the same.

"There's not much time," the other self said, twitched a smile.

"Jaguar," Jadis said.

The other self nodded. "I've taken the liberty of preparing the med-kit." She raised the leg of her pants to reveal a puckered mass of flesh from an old wound. "It *will* heal." She let the pant leg fall back. "Key Jaguar into the com. Everything you need to know will be there." Her other self gestured to Jadis. "I'm sorry but you'll have to haul yourself out of there. If we touch – "

"– It will cause some kind of time problem."

Jaguar nodded again. "Hurry."

Jadis managed to gather her limbs under herself and hobbled out of the lift, dizzy as if she'd been drugged. In the next moment her other self was in the lift and gone.

Disorientation fled. What was left was a profound sense of numbness; for long minutes she leaned against the wall, staring at where she'd seen herself disappear. And then urgency returned when pain leaked through her senses.

A dressing to keep the wound clean was all that was necessary. Laser-fire came about as antiseptic as it got, and there had been no blood because of cauterization. The wound did throb, to the point she acquiesced to the painkiller her other self had prepared – not an injection as she'd thought, rather an herbal remedy that cooled and soothed the moment she pressed the concoction to her calf. She couldn't help but wonder how much she was to learn in the years ahead.

While she did this she watched a holo of herself spin a yarn as fantastic as anything she'd heard, so fantastic that it had to be believable. So many twists. So much tampering with time.

Originally Jadis had been drugged during that recent dinner. Why, had been not as she thought, not to kill her. Amaru had time-lifted her to the future, exiling her to a life from which he thought she'd never be able to escape and so forever silence her. He forgot, however, with whom he was dealing. Not only did she override all his security codes in the lifts, but used his own credits to travel backwards and forwards through time, all the while sabotaging his operations, guided by facts Erdoes had told her long ago. That had been a cleverly crafted plan. Not only had she time-lifted Amaru's precious shipments of water to the same location, but arranged it so that all the containers were no longer in existence in the past. All that arrived in the past was water. Water that spilled out to the ground and worked its way back into the water table.

The blinks Jadis had seen were the result of time interference.

"Remember never underestimate your prey," the holo said, blue eyes bright. For a moment Jadis felt as if she were looking directly at herself, a real person, not some recorded projection of light. "It's something we've done too often with Amaru."

Jadis nodded. Her holo told her of how Amaru had parried brilliantly. As time was simultaneous, he lifted back to the point before that fateful dinner, had all the drugs substituted and again replayed that evening, this time sending Jadis on a mission to hunt herself.

Now would come the counter-feint.

She transferred all this information to Abram just as insurance. Her own records were wiped clean and she smashed the hard drive as an extra precaution.

She contacted Amaru.

"You didn't say if you wanted a clay," she said before he could even utter a greeting. At that moment she was glad she'd had the communication holoed. For the first time he'd see her in her working clothes, and the effect she knew would not be without impact. It was worth it to see his face harden. "But I've made one anyway," she added.

"Really."

She could almost feel him chew that word.

"Really. But it'll be a year before I have another exhibition so you might as well pick it up now." She smiled. It was all teeth and no tenderness. "Credit my account triple the usual amount. I'll wait."

"Where is it? – the clay?"

"Here. Where else would I have it?"

"It might have been – "

"At the gallery? Don't be dense. Why would I let Abram see this one?"

That got his attention. "I'll lift right over."

"Not until my account's been credited."

"Bitch!"

She grinned. "As you wish."

But he did it and then she made her next move – a program change in the com so that she could control the lift from a remote, and then she left.

Back at the main camp it was plain her other self had completed the first phase of their plan. Not a guard was in sight, no personnel; as a matter of fact not even any buildings were to be seen. Only the lift remained. Everything else had been destroyed in the past.

When Jadis stepped away from the grey cylinder she laughed at the absurdity of that sight. Everywhere there was forest, green and fragrant, and here, stuck like some ponderous mushroom, was a lift. The lamp post awaiting Mr. Tumnus.

Her fingers played over the controls. She had no sooner finished when the indicator blinked. He was coming.

Anger hardened his face when he materialized. She motioned him out of the lift.

"What's the meaning of this?"

Again she made a gesture, this time for him to walk ahead of her. As she thought he might, he slipped a gun from his tunic and it was on the ground before he could even think of firing. She'd broken his hand in the bargain. But it cost her. Her leg seared again.

"Go." And again she gestured to the forest.

This time he did as he was told, nursing his hand, his eyes cold. She offered him not another word and he made no attempt to ply her for information. Only bird song marked their passage.

When they reached Crane Lake she let the shock of the scene hit him. None of the pipes fed into the water. All had gone, a trick Jaguar had performed while meddling with time. And there, at the shore, stood a terra cotta of herself, dark against the arms of the birch. Another trick her other self had performed.

Amaru's gaze fired to her, back to the clay, his mouth parting in question.

"This *is* the right hit," she said, controlling her extreme sense of disorientation.

His golden complexion paled. Perhaps the bushmaster tasted his own venom.

"Yes." He paced toward the sculpture, his fingers trembling when he reached for it, touched it, dropped away.

She smiled. "So you *did* know Jaguar."

He still stared at the sculpture. "What?"

"You knew the identity of Jaguar."

He whirled. Caught.

In that moment the clay exploded and a figure of black lunged, pulling Amaru down into the water. Rings of silver pooled out along that flat sheet of green, grew to a boil, subsided. It was some moments before two bodies bobbed to the surface, backs to the swath of blue sky.

Jadis bent to her heels and let the coldness of the moment overwhelm her, letting Erdoes' howl wail through her one last time. If ever there was a hell it was to see your own death, and now that hell would be forever with her.

Erdoes had been right. She *did* have to care. Perhaps it was worth living with hell knowing this place was free of Amaru.

She stood, turned her face to the forest, letting its vibrancy heal the place Erdoes had left.

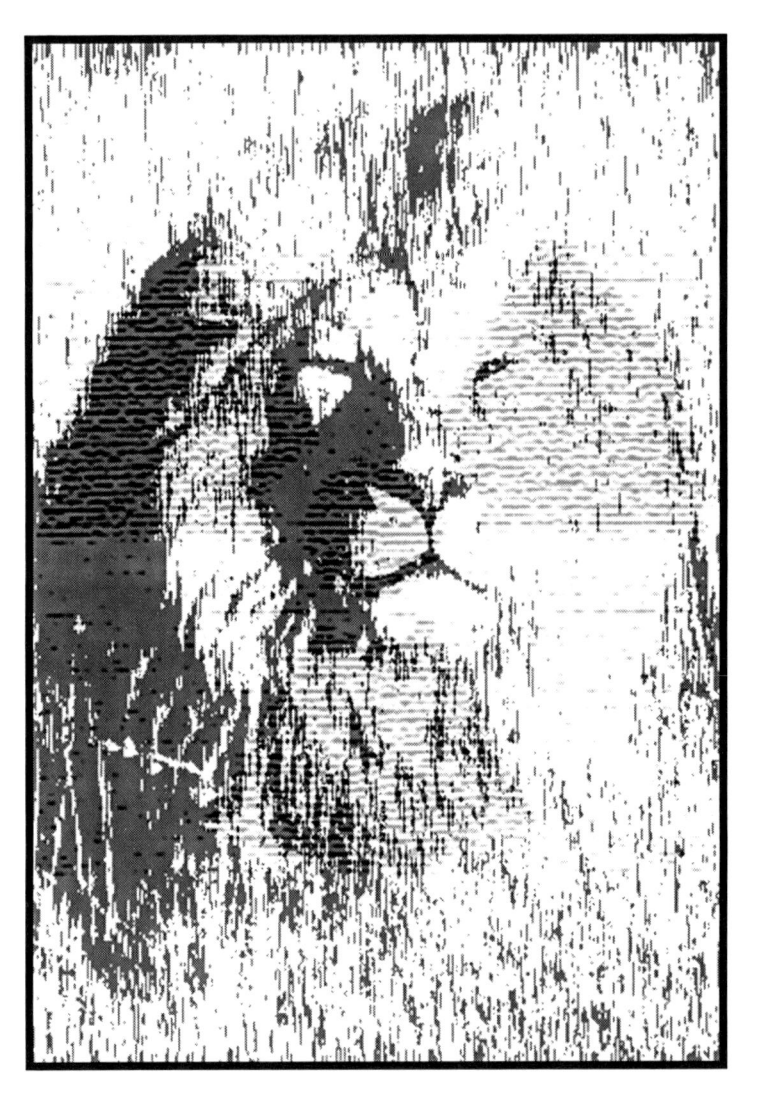

Figure 12: Digital painting, Lorina Stephens

The Green Season

There were only two colours to the world: gold of the plains, blue of the sky. Zebra grazed upon the gold, antelope among them. At a few copses and trees I could see giraffe, tall and lovely, although the aunts would have disapproved of finding beauty in food. Ibis were there, strolling on stick legs through the herds, other birds riding the backs of zebras.

The only thing to mar the scene was the ruin at the lake's edge. It was the lake that bound us all together, whether food or predator, and the ruin that reminded me of a past that was forbidden. White, like bones bleached, each season the buildings of the humans slid away in the winds and crumbled in the sun.

My attention shifted to the pride, to where the aunts lolled, panting against the heat, to the younglings ignorant in their sleep of the flies that harried them. The young males, three of them, lay in a huddle sharing whispers.

And then to Kgosi. He was sweet, and ancient, and full of tales of his youth – conquests and failures, wonder and sorrow – and I loved him more than I should. Like the others he slept, although I always had the feeling he merely closed his eyes and that his mind raced on through scenes more fantastic than I could ever hope to dream.

I should have been sleeping like the others. Youngling naps long ago disinterested me, and to lie among the aunts was something I hadn't yet earned. It was only with Kgosi I felt I had a place.

My chance came finally. The last carcass had been stolen by hyenas and there was pressure for another kill, or a steal. Adaeze left with four of the other aunts, leaving Chipo to care for the younglings.

I finessed my escape by tumbling with the younglings in a way that took me farther and farther from Chipo, closer and closer to Kgosi.

I attacked his ears. He growled. I dove before him and rolled to my back, offering him my neck. A lick welcomed me. We set to our usual grooming with dispatch.

When at last inaction took us we simply lay beside one another, I gathered my courage and asked, "Will you tell me again of the humans?"

I could feel him tense. He turned, locating Chipo, denial for an answer.

Such frustration. I longed for him to tell me again how the humans had given us language, how they were powerful and marvellous and filled with knowledge more than I could hope to attain.

Instead I studied the creatures on the plain – the bowing, the sniffing, the way their bodies spoke the words they could not.

"But why don't the aunts teach us these things?" I asked.

"It has nothing to do with survival."

Indeed. I had learned what the humans taught us died with our forbearers, slowly, bits and bits falling away until what was forgotten was greater than what was remembered, this under the pressure of surviving.

I thought of the ruins to the south, the place Kgosi said he'd visited. There was knowledge for which I hungered, and in a rush of words I told him I would go.

"You will not."

"But I –"

"You will not. There is death for those who find those places."

"But you're not dead."

He looked down at me then, his amber eyes soft, fluid, like suns in the warmth they radiated to me. "The human places cause a wasting. I am wasting. I will die."

"So will we all."

"But not as I." I started to protest but he silenced me with a look. "I have seen it happen. All of us who visited the human places have died. First come the lumps, then comes the wasting, death last."

"But surely this is knowledge the pride should have –"

"It is forbidden."

"Forbidden. The aunts can't see that you're wise."

"There will be a time you will come to hold me in contempt." His great head bobbed, indicating the aunts. "As they hold me in contempt."

"But I love you –"

"And you may still in the end. But you will also learn of contempt."

He nuzzled me. That small act of affection filled me with sorrow, the fear that I might betray him and yet still he would love me, forgive me for what I would have to do as an aunt. This for the well-being of the pride.

Chipo found me, snarled, lunged, nicking my foreleg. "Talking is for the males."

I winced at the blows in her voice. Such condemnation. She compared me to the young males who talked and talked and endlessly talked and did nothing to contribute to the pride.

Her threat was clear: These things of which Kgosi spoke wouldn't feed us. They wouldn't protect us. They wouldn't stand us in good stead in the season without rain when the young would come and the pride depend upon the strength of the aunts.

Linger, and I would be outcast.

Under the pressure of Chipo's warning I unwrapped myself from what Kgosi offered, feeling the loss of his company. I scrambled away into the chaos of the younglings. She left off her attack. But I was under her scrutiny for several hours.

There was no successful hunt that day. Or the next. During that time I often attempted to seek out Kgosi. Always the aunts stood between us. What hurt more was that he not once stirred himself to find my company. Had he done something overt to shun me I could have at least felt betrayed. But I knew nothing of how to react to his apathy.

Finally Adaeze and the other aunts returned with an antelope. Kgosi was given his fill first. They moved in when he was barely clear of the kill. I gorged on what remained, with the other younglings who had taken to tooth.

After that there was nothing to do but snooze and play.

I'd caught a mouse, fully aware I had something the other younglings wanted. Just as I expected, one of them tried to best me for it. I boxed her soundly. Another tried. And another. It was simple to defeat them, being older, stronger, and in an attempt to sweeten the game, and my own comfort, I said, "Whoever brings me the best, the softest feathers can have the mouse."

First I was brought a feather, very pretty, very blue. But it was, after all, only a feather. I ignored the offering. Another dumped a mouthful of soggy feathers at my paws. These for my mouse?

I turned my head away in disgust.

Finally one of them brought me an ibis. Clever youngling. I accepted the ibis – it was a lot of feathers and a lot of meat – and exchanged it for my mouse.

The aunts pounced upon us at that moment. Adaeze grabbed my neck. This was no play. I rolled to my back, obeisant. Still she attacked. Distantly I could hear mewling, coughs, screams.

Of course. I should have known better. This wasn't a game the aunts would approve. This had been something from the time of humans.

The Green Season

Pain brought me back to my attacker. With a final slash at my ears she stepped away.

"We are lions," she said.

"We are superior lions," I retorted.

She lunged for my throat again. I stilled. Again she retreated.

"I could kill you for heresy."

I remained upon my back. "But we were given a gift –"

"–that is nothing more than a bane. Individuals will not be tolerated."

Again the threat of exile.

"She's inexperienced," Kgosi said.

The aunts rounded on him. He snarled, but he backed away.

They left us with parting blows. I lost both my mouse and my ibis.

Even so I caught what Adaeze said to my mother-aunt: "The green season is coming upon us."

Why, I wondered, did that forecast thunder through me?

And why did my mother-aunt throw me that knowing look?

I was to know the answer to that when at last the green season came. By then we'd moved south, prepared for the torrents that came every year, a tree for a home. The land here flattened into true plains, unlike the rolling countryside of our northern home. Trees were few, wider than tall, seeded in that long-forgotten time when humans had been with us. What grew beneath the trees were mostly thin grasses and sedges, yellow when the rains failed, brilliant green when they came.

And so the rains came. It always happened all of a sudden. One day land so dry it puffed beneath your paws. The next there was oozing mud, cool after so much heat. It was during the rains the bowl of our shallow lake filled, fed by streams rushing down from the mountains.

A pathetic lot we were – wet through, fur matted, balancing tempers and conditions as best we were able, and while the tension of this sang through my body, day upon day, I heard the message in the rain. Insistent. Tormenting. Beating upon my head until I felt I would bolt. But I didn't bolt. I only sat there like the aunts, listening to something only newly apparent. It drummed upon our heads. It grew around our feet. Within days the message was there for us all to see. Growth. Rebirth.

It was time for the living.

The yellow plains became that vibrant green. Antelope and gazelle sprang over the grass, zebra braying and kicking. At the water's edge ibis pecked, plucking fish which were now abundant and came from who knows where. The smell was overwhelming – rich, sickly sweet.

And the Angels Sang

The fecund earth was new to me this year, new as it had not been last year. Had it been this vital last season? Surely not. I couldn't remember this vibrancy in my limbs, this urgency pushing me toward....

What? I had no idea.

"What is this?" I asked finally of my mother-aunt, offering her the proper obeisance.

She nuzzled my cheek, her breath hot. "It is the green season."

And that was all.

"But, please, there must be –"

Her paw swatted my ears. I ducked, missing the pain.

I skulked away to a subordinate place where I could escape the tension around the aunts, watching, watching, always watching for some clue upon the grasslands. The gazelle fed in the distance, some of them mounting others. Zebra were likewise engaged. My attention slipped to the ibis that were contorting themselves into bizarre rituals – bobbing, twisting their necks, unfurling long wings. There were no others my age to ask. I had been the only child from that breeding season, and for me to ask those younger would have proved fruitless, and to ask the young males was impossible.

Hours dragged into days. The aunts took down a gazelle. There was meat that night. Through all of it their tension rose. They touched each other little. Grooming often turned into arguments. Even Kgosi paced, throwing sidelong glances in our direction. That afternoon the aunts attacked the young males, driving them from the pride. I watched the youngling males. Ignorant they were. They had no idea what waited for them.

On the fourth day, in the ebb of the rains, one of the aunts rose, sinuous, powerful in a way I couldn't remember, and strode to where Kgosi paced. He paused, watching her. I could feel the hunger in his gaze, a hunger which had nothing to do with food.

Four of the others followed, all aunts with weaned younglings. Eshe, a small aunt, nudged me toward the others. Without a word we set off across the plain, travelling through the day and into the night, and just as we set off we stopped, in the middle of nowhere. We slept. No one said anything. I had no idea why we had come so far, or why we were here.

"I don't understand," I whispered to Eshe.

She only smiled and answered, "It's the green season," rolled over and left me to ask the stars.

The tension in the aunts was as real as a cry. It did everything to affect me so that by the time Eshe and the four aunts rose, I was pacing, hungering for something I couldn't name, our smell filling my nose, my mouth, intoxicating and maddening. The tension wasn't in the trees. It wasn't in the grass.

The aunts ringed Kgosi. I followed out of impulse. Somehow I felt distanced, as if I watched myself from afar.

The others were all bright-eyed, watching Kgosi who stared at us. Did he, also, feel these new things?

Eshe was the first to break the stillness. She did something that troubled me. She moved to Kgosi, brushing against his flank. He growled, lunged for her. Deftly, she slid away, rolled down to her back and moaned. I wondered at this behaviour, wondered at its meaning. He answered, low, throaty, and this also was out of character for him.

Still she wound around him. By now others of the aunts rose, dancing their dance until the very air shuddered with the smell of their excitement. It was delicious, a new awareness. It demanded something of me. And I heard. Watching them touch and roll, smell and lick, vie for his attention, I knew I wanted his attention in a way different from what we'd shared.

Drawn by this thing, I joined their dance. I was clumsy at first. But the power of it caught me and taught me. I dipped to the ground beneath his feet, offering my belly in deference, spreading my legs so he would smell the excitement of what I felt.

It was Adaeze who had him first. He sprang across me, almost ignorant of me. Adaeze crouched upon her belly, her tail high. Even from where I lay I could see the swollen flesh, pink. In the next moment he was over her. I couldn't remember seeing him this way, powerful, gripping her neck between his massive jaws. This wasn't the Kgosi I knew. But he was the Kgosi I wanted – Kgosi the male.

Their coupling was quick. She snarled and turned on him when he withdrew. Painful? For a moment the thought this exquisite dance might end in pain was daunting. But the smell of the aunts pulled me back into instinct.

I approached Kgosi again. Again he ignored me and coupled with one of the other aunts. Over and over he stepped by me as though I were invisible, driving my need to have him until I knew I'd never be able to control what I felt.

I was the last he approached. It was a beginning, and it was also an ending. He mounted my back, his breath hot on my neck when he said, "Remember that I loved you when you can feel for me nothing but contempt," and then I sank into the pleasure and the pain he gave me.

The breeding continued for days. By its end Kgosi lay at some distance from the aunts, his sides quivering.

"He will give us weaklings this season," Eshe said. Murmurs of agreement passed through them like a condemnation and suddenly I was filled with dread my youngling would be abandoned for its deformity.

That was my first iniquity: that I should despise Kgosi for his weakened sperm.

We returned to the pride quickly, as strangely as we set out. There was a fresh kill, and an odd silence as we all took our share. Nothing was said about the breeding until the next day – what would happen within my body, the signs to watch for, what to do. The aunts taught me as they always did – one by one, in bits and bits.

I soon forgot my transgression against Kgosi when I knew I'd conceived. Of the five of us, I was the only one to bear, something of which I was jealously proud.

The season of green faded into the season of ochre. My hunting forays with the aunts were growing less successful as the game moved. The southern lake dried, no more than a vast mud hole now. Fish had been flapping in the wallows for days. The stink of death was in the drying grass. And so we began our migration to the north.

This early in the dry season the northern lake to which we came was vast, still lush. We ate a lot while the eating was good, often gorging to the point we were incapable of doing anything but sleep. Kgosi, however, ate less and less.

I did my share, thinking of the lean time. Often I threw myself into the shade, panting in the heat. Kgosi lay near, watching, and when the aunts were busy with themselves or the hunt we groomed one another.

Somehow things had changed between us – he cautious, I preoccupied with what grew in my belly. It was while grooming him my tongue caught upon a lump behind his ear – soft, like the bladder of a gazelle. He winced. We said nothing and I avoided the area, yet both of us knew this was the beginning of the wasting.

I had been out on a foray with Eshe and Adaeze when we first caught wind of two males. We crouched in the yellow grass, downwind. They circled our encampment, sniffing, bending to one another in conversation.

"What are they doing?" I asked Adaeze.

"Watching."

As if I couldn't see that. "What are they watching?"

"Kgosi."

There could be only one reason they watched him. They meant to take his place. I'd heard of these things.

Panic filled me. I turned away to warn him. Adaeze leapt upon me, pinning me under her jaws.

"You can't tell him."

"But he needs to know!"

"He needs to know nothing. If Kgosi is worthy of his place among us he will hold it. If not ...." She let the sentence dangle.

I turned to Eshe for support. There was none to be had there.

"Don't you love him at all?"

They looked at one another as if I had asked them for a miracle, and then Adaeze answered, "Love has nothing to do with this. This is survival."

Always survival. It was the credo of the aunts.

I shook off Adaeze's hold and glared at her. It was as effective as when I challenged her as a youngling - all show and toothless. For a moment I understood how Kgosi must feel.

We moved away toward our prey, keeping distance between ourselves and the males. I was to take the place of the third runner, being heavy, Adaeze and Eshe taking first and second. It would be my responsibility to deliver the suffocating hold.

A young weakling was spotted in the gazelle herd, straying. Adaeze broke into a run, Eshe behind her. It took me a moment to follow. All I could think of was Kgosi. Even when Adaeze and Eshe brought the poor thing down, and I cut off its wind, my thoughts were with him, wondering if the males had challenged him yet, if he would be victorious.

I dragged our kill back myself. As the subordinate one, these tasks were mine. Had it been a year earlier I might have challenged that. Now I had a youngling to consider.

There was talk and talk when we returned, the whole camp in an uproar. One of the aunts chased the younglings, trying to herd them. The elder aunts were in a council circle, their faces grave.

Instantly my attention was for Kgosi. He lay at a distance, as always, but his sides heaved. I longed to go to him. The aunts prevented that, calling me into the council circle.

"There has been an attempt to overthrow the male," Chipo said. She might have been discussing the day's food for all the emotion in her voice.

"Yet he lives," Adaeze said.

All eyes flicked to where Kgosi lay. They had no need to say it for me to hear: He only barely lived.

"Shouldn't we tend his wounds?" I asked.

All eyes turned to me. I longed to slink away from the accusation on their faces.

"He is the only male we have," I said.

They glanced at one another. They knew as well as I the young males who had challenged him would have put distance between themselves and us.

"Do it," Adaeze said at last.

I let go a breath and left them.

He barely acknowledged me when I sat beside him. There was a long gash from his cheek to his mouth. This would heal if I kept it clean. It was the other wounds I couldn't see that bothered me. To have left him to die would have been wise. There were always younger males,

But as I looked at him struggling for breath, all I could remember were his words when we mated in the green season.

Although I jeopardized the pride by doing what I did, I bathed his wounds with my tongue, smelling his body to see what else had been done in his struggle to keep his place among us. There was nothing I could detect, or knew how to detect, yet here was the smell of death around him.

I left him in the shade of our tree and returned to the kill to select him some choice bits.

Adaeze boxed my ears. "None for him."

I lunged and let my teeth sink into her back. Blood spattered, wet on my muzzle. She rounded on me. This time it was I who caught her on her belly.

"I'm acting for the pride," I said, as flatly and calmly as I could.

She growled, her eyes narrowing. It was her threat that was toothless this time. She wouldn't dare endanger the only female to conceive this season.

Her gaze dropped. She backed away. I bent to the kill and pulled free the pieces I wanted and took them to Kgosi.

He was unable to eat what I brought him as it was. I chewed the meat first and gave him the pulp from my mouth, feeding him like a youngling just come to tooth. He did nothing to protest. He only gave me a weak nudge.

For several weeks I continued to care for him. All the while my belly grew heavier until the weight of what I carried was almost more than I could bear. Often when I would sit with Kgosi, he would nuzzle my round belly, pleased when the youngling would kick.

It was on one such occasion that my nipples began to drip. He licked away the fluid and purred, wincing at the effort.

"Soon now," he said. "The youngling will come soon."

Only a few days later the pains began and I walked out of our encampment, knowing this was something I would have to do for myself. I paused only when the pain became acute, stealing my breath and blinding my eyes. In a gush my water broke. Still I kept walking, searching for a place we would be safe.

When finally I found a place among the scrub, I could barely see for the pain, wanting only to push away this agony. All at once the pain ended, and somehow I was left feeling abandoned, empty. Yet I wasn't abandoned. There at my tail lay a youngling still wet in afterbirth. I licked her clean, tasting the blood and salt and then later her own body. She cried. I licked. Again she cried and it was a good sound, strong, healthy. Carefully I nudged her to my belly and brought her to feed. For as long as I live I will never feel quite so content as I did at that moment, feeling the pull of her mouth upon my nipple, watching her small mouth move.

The following day I returned to the pride, carrying my youngling in my mouth. Beneath the banyan lay Kgosi, sleeping. The aunts were some distance from him, surrounded on every side by the gazelle, the antelope and the zebra that grazed upon the dying grass.

I broke our own laws yet again and dropped my youngling at Kgosi's paws. He rumbled in that satisfied way and set to a serious grooming of his new daughter.

The other aunts came upon us quickly. We were acknowledged with the usual rubbings and smellings. Now I was given a place in the shade among the aunts, no longer relegated to lay by myself in the heat of the sun.

There was a naming a few days later. Dambudzo. We came to call her Dambudzo, which meant *Trouble*.

Kgosi was proud of her and held her between his paws, purring walking songs he had discovered from that long-ago race of humans. The weeks passed and these lengthened into months. Mostly I was left to care for the younglings while the aunts foraged for food, and I was happy enough to do this, letting one or the other feed from my nipples. My milk flowed too heavily and too freely for Dambudzo alone. Often, while we were alone, Kgosi would bend toward me and feed also, a thing of which I knew the aunts would not approve. But I allowed him. He was so thin and I wouldn't see him suffer.

The aunts found us all together, the younglings sleeping around us. They may have disapproved. I didn't care.

The dry season lengthened, parched; the lake grew smaller daily so that disputes and battles occurred often. The antelope were the first to leave. Then the gazelle, the zebra, migrating to the lowlands where the rains would come again.

Once more we moved. Three of the young died along the way, unable to keep the pace the aunts set. Although I didn't like it, I understood. We couldn't afford to keep weaklings. The survival of the pride depended upon our strength.

I was glad little Dambudzo was as robust as she was. There had been moments I worried, wondering if the fact she was the only child of the last green season would have anything to do with her health.

When the rains came again I chose not to go to the breeding. Dambudzo was young and my body was still adjusting. Five others went. After several days five aunts returned, Kgosi lagging behind. He had remained so thin since that attack in the northlands. The look on his face filled me with foreboding.

Our days passed as always – hunting, feeding, teaching the younglings. The males of age were driven out of the pride. And we waited for a sign in the cycles of the breeding aunts.

And waited.

And no sign came.

Whispers stirred among us: Kgosi was too old. The pride couldn't continue. I think perhaps he understood this, because he kept a greater distance from us than usual, only mildly interested in the play of the younglings.

Even I worried. Without a strong male in the pride, we were prey to any marauding bands of younger males on the plains. Dambudzo would be endangered.

There was only one alternative for us: to find a male capable of holding a position among us. Younglings would be conceived. The pride would continue.

The arguments sounded so reasonable. When the two males who had stalked Kgosi in the dry season appeared once more, it was I who went out to them, inviting them into the pride.

The challenge to Kgosi was issued the following day. He rose unsteadily. I caught his attention just as he turned to face the two young males and I inhaled sharply. There had been such forgiveness on his face.

I turned away, trying to soothe the ache that filled me. All I could remember were his words to me: *Remember that I loved you when you can feel for me nothing but contempt.*

He didn't even fight. They killed him with the first blow, and I clutched Dambudzo tightly, moaning against her soft fur.

Cool, deliberate, the one called Abrafo yanked Dambudzo from my paws and snapped her neck. I growled and lunged, pulled off him by Adaeze and another aunt. They both held me even when the males killed the other younglings. Not one of the aunts did anything to save their children. I thought I would never stop screaming, and I thought I would never stop wanting to kill them.

It was then I learned of contempt. For the new males to establish their places among us they had to breed and clear the younglings. I had not known this.

It rained that night, long and heavy and completely relentless, and in the rain I wept. I wept for Dambudzo. I wept for Kgosi. And I wept for the things that I had lost.

The next day the breeding began again. I, like the others who had lost their younglings, went to fill my womb with life. It was a breeding. It had nothing to do with love. And it had everything to do with life. Even in that moment when the male called Amrapmoi entered me, my thoughts were of a time when the land was green and Kgosi and I lay with Dambudzo between us.

Figure 13: Watercolour and digital painting, Lorina Stephens

Figure 14: Pen & ink sketch, Peter MacDougall, previously published On Spec, Vol. 7 No. 4 (#23) Winter, 1995
http://www3.telus.net/pem/tea.htm

For a Cup of Tea

Published previously, On Spec, Vol. 7 No. 4 (#23) Winter, 1995

It was a foolish wager, Captain Robertson Giles Malvern knew. A thousand British pounds on the faith of his crew and the love of a ship stretched the limits of propriety. But that strutting ass of a captain aboard *Thermopylae* put his balls in an uproar. As if that tug could beat *Cutty Sark* into the Thames docks. Even in light winds between London and Shanghai she'd made the voyage in 104 days, and consistently brought in the best prices for tea.

As the last of her cargo descended into the hold Malvern observed the Shanghai docks.

There was no smell quite like Shanghai, no spectacle quite so enthralling. Shanghai was like opium. It could give you everything. It could rob you of everything. Now he'd gone and made that wager. Fool man that he was. If he lost he'd be ruined.

First mate, Greaves Hardstrom, strode abreast. "Hold's secured, Captain," he said. "I hear there's been a wager."

"Aye," Malvern grunted. A boy by the boarding gate caught his attention, his attire too opulent for a wharf rat: black silk tunic and pants edged in gold. The boy's dark hair was tied in a queue and gleamed in the sun. Altogether a very beautiful Chinese face. It occurred to Malvern this boy would have a hard time among the scurvy knaves of Shanghai's streets.

The boy stood beside a brass jar that was unusual even to Malvern. Easily five feet tall, it reached to the boy's shoulder, a relief of fire demons and citadels circling the belly of the thing. Its mouth was sealed in wood, red wax and brass grips. As impressive as the boy.

Hardstrom laughed, pulling back Malvern's attention. "The crew's agreed to back you on your wager. Matter of pride, you might say."

Pride indeed. "With luck we'll be in port by the end of March."

"End of March nothing, Captain. We'll be there afore the middle."

Malvern smiled at Hardstrom's boast, knowing it well-founded. "All in order then?"

For a Cup of Tea

"Ready as soon as one last matter's dealt with." With a nod Hardstrom indicated the young boy standing by the boarding gate. "We've a passenger. The boy's papers are all in order." Hardstrom handed them to the captain.

"Li Tu-hsiu?" He shot the boy a look. "A courier for the Emperor?"

Hardstrom gestured to the enormous brass bottle. "And that's what he's delivering to the London Museum."

"What's in the bottle?"

"The boy assures me nothing to harm the crew."

That seemed a careful way of putting it, Malvern thought. He shoved the papers back to the first mate. "Have him bunked as far from the rest of the crew as possible."

With a wave for a salute, Hardstrom lumbered off toward the boy. Malvern decided the boy was altogether much too feminine to survive in Shanghai's streets.

"Secured, sir," Hardstrom shouted up the deck. Captain Brown aboard Thermopylae bellowed across the water, "I hope you're a man who honours his debts, Malvern!"

Thermopylae's crew made ready. Malvern clenched his fists. "Get her underway, Mr. Hardstrom!" he roared. *Cutty Sark's* sails thundered out. In mid-harbour her jibs unfurled, luffed, were trimmed and then bellied. Thermopylae's crew jeered. "Fly the mains!" Malvern ordered. Canvas cracked against the breeze. Men heaved the lines. The bow came about. Almost hull to hull both clippers turned to starboard, but slowly, perceptibly, *Cutty Sark* eased away. Brown could be heard barking commands.

Let him bark, Malvern thought. *Cutty Sark's* royals now cupped the wind. When they sailed into Formosa Strait, Malvern felt a distinct sense of pleasure as he watched *Thermopylae* shrink behind. His pleasure dimmed when he spied the boy upon the aft deck. Nineteen, he'd place him. Nineteen and a pack of trouble, he was sure. What in the name of God was this boy doing aboard his ship? Working his fingers in those odd shapes?

He grunted and strode off to his navigator.

By evening, there wasn't even a silhouette of *Thermopylae* on the horizon.

๑๏๑

Malvern, fussy on the subject of custom, would have made an exception and pleaded work, even illness, to have excused himself from dining with his aristocratic passenger, but the question of prevarication rankled even more. At the moment he presided over ocean perch, peas and mounds of mashed potatoes.

And the Angels Sang

First Mate Hardstrom just asked the navigator - a thin, frail man by name of Long - when they'd be passing through Sunda Straight.

"About thirty-one days, I'd expect," Long answered, "if these winds hold."

"Aye," Second Mate Petersen, next to him, said, "and we'll be leaving *Thermopylae* well behind."

"I understand there's been a wager," Li Tu-hsiu said in flawless English.

Malvern shot his guest a glance. "It won't interfere with your journey."

"I didn't mean to suggest it would." Li's wrists rested against the table, his pale ivory arms disappearing into extravagant folds of red silk. Overhead, a lantern swung ponderously, casting odd shadows around his eyes. "I was merely curious."

"There's nothing about which to be curious, Mr. Tu-hsiu. *Cutty Sark* will be into port long before *Thermopylae*."

"Should you require any assistance...." Li smiled.

Malvern snorted. "Shanghai bribery doesn't work at sea."

"I wasn't speaking of bribing bureaucrats."

"Then bribery of what?" the ship's surgeon asked.

Li looked at the surgeon. Without so much as a smirk or a laugh, he answered, "Spirits."

It was perhaps because of Li's seriousness not an officer scoffed. Malvern couldn't help remembering the invective Hardstrom had thrown at the sea-witch in a long-ago battle with death: *Nanny, my life's forfeit if you'll just save Malvern!*

And now they both rode a ship named for the short shift she wore.

"There's no need for carnival entertainment aboard my ship," Malvern said, speaking with more conviction than he felt.

"I assure you I spoke not of entertainment."

"Are you claiming the state of prestidigitator?" the ship's surgeon asked, winking at the second mate next to him.

"A man of science should be careful about forming uninformed conclusions."

"And I suppose you'll tell us that jai's some sort of djinni?"

"Effreeti, actually, a long-ago gift from a visiting Ceylonese potentate."

The men laughed with derision. Malvern clenched his jaw, thinking of ways to redirect this conversation.

"Right then," the ship's surgeon said, "Mr. Li Tu-hsiu, I'm waiting for some evidence you're what you claim."

"I believe you already have that."

Malvern asked, "And what is that?"

"Have you seen *Thermopylae* anywhere near?"

"That's just fine sailing from a fine clipper," Hardstrom said.

For a Cup of Tea

Li pivoted back toward the men. His attention was on Hardstrom, slid down to the first mate's plate where there were only the bones of the ocean perch.

Had it not been for fair weather, Malvern would have sworn those bones moved from the sway of the clipper. Those bones moved again. More now. Filaments of white spun from rib to rib, the grey-white scales sweeping back from what should have been a lifeless head but that the gills now pulsed, once, twice, a third time. In the next moment a whole, very alive fish flopped against the china, arced onto its back and flipped sideways, smashing crystal and tumbling silver as it fell to the floor.

As Hardstrom bent, all at the same time, to seize this impossibility, bones hit the floor where a gasping fish had been for the briefest moment.

Malvern lurched to his feet. "I'll not have any of your dark arts aboard my ship. Is that clear?"

Li swung round to meet him. "Infinitely, Captain. Shall I remove the enchantment I've put upon the ship?"

"Yes, damn you!"

"I thought you wanted to win?"

"I do, but in a fair race!"

"What makes you think this is a fair race?"

"Because for whatever else Brown may be, he is fair."

"Has it occurred to you there are other interests here?"

"What other interests could there be?"

"Those of the Empress Tz'u Hsi and the Emperor Hsien-feng."

Hardstrom rose to confront Li who still sat, implacable, very much the face of China. "What interest would they have in a wager between two English captains?"

"The Empress was very much annoyed when the Emperor announced my charge as a gift to the London Museum."

"So?"

"So news, such as the wager between Captains Brown and Malvern, is often of interest to the Empress. She saw an opportunity –"

"And being the dragon lady she is, seized it," Hardstrom said, passing Malvern a look. "If she can't have the precious jar she'll see it's delivered ruined."

Malvern asked Li, "Is that about it?"

"Almost. Indeed the Empress wants to see you ruined for having obstructed her wishes, inadvertently though that might have been. But she also wants the effreeti."

"And knowing the Empress she's loaded this wager in her favour."

"Very much. It was for that very reason the Emperor entrusted the care of the effreeti bottle to me. Should the Empress seize it – "

"She'd use the effreeti for her own purposes."

"Plans within plans. The Manchu dynasty hasn't retained power by being squeamish." Li glanced around the room at the men. "And the Empress is very much part of that dynasty. Just as the Emperor has placed his most trusted magician into play, so has the Empress."

"*Thermopylae* has a passenger," Hardstrom said.

"A passenger who's no doubt a magician," Malvern finished.

"Indeed. Do you still wish me to lift my spell?"

"No."

Malvern stalked from the mess – both the room and the situation.

ஓ

So. It was to be an unfair race involving magic and royalty spoiled on indulgence and power.

As Malvern did every day since leaving Shanghai, he cursed that monster of a boy who dropped spells willy-nilly aboard his ship, who threatened the deadly balance he'd forged with whatever god, or spirit, or thing, that had allowed him to live because of Hardstrom's defiance. Checks and balances. Deftly kept. Now all threatened.

Thermopylae entered Sunda Straight with them past midday. The winds slackened. For several hours *Cutty Sark* ran in full sail, spreading as much canvas as possible to catch the fickle winds. Even with that boy twitching spells upon the bow, *Cutty Sark* only inched forward. He lost sight of *Thermopylae* by sunset.

He ordered Li brought forward. "What seems to be the problem?"

Li bowed. "Problem, Captain?"

"She's pulling away."

"I had noticed."

"You said you were a magician."

"And I also said they had a magician. Just like the wind, there are bound to be lifts and falls to power."

"You're saying he's more powerful than you?"

"Don't be foolish. He's merely gained an edge while I rest."

"Rest? Do you see my crew resting? Will this wager rest?"

"No and no. But if you want to win this race you'll have to trust me."

Trust him? No farther than he could throw him. He dismissed Li with a grunt and a scowl. For the remainder of the day Malvern stood spread-stance upon the forecastle, watching the horizon.

For a Cup of Tea

By dawn fatigue lines fanned his already wrinkled eyes and his crew muttered a little more loudly. That was something he wouldn't have and gave orders to swab the deck, to adjust the course and to refine the sails. Shortly after that the breezes freshened. A cheer coursed over the decks. Even cooky came above and beat the rail with a copper ladle.

All that halted when Li made an appearance. Malvern turned to where the crew looked.

The boy was pale, his eyes glazed as if seeing into a world none of them could comprehend. To the side of him, Malvern saw one of the men crossing himself. Li staggered to the port rail, pushed his way along until he stood near Malvern. One hand continually worked through the same gesture, slight, like a twitch, tracing an endless circle with an S curve through the middle. Yin and Yang.

More balances? Malvern wondered at this.

He ordered cooky to bring the boy tea, a pot of it, to set it on deck. When it arrived, steaming and aromatic, he poured and offered the cup to Li. Li made no acknowledgment and simply kept his left hand sweeping through that gesture.

"Can you hear me?" Malvern asked.

Li nodded slightly.

"Is there a problem?"

Li shook his head.

"Do you need assistance?"

Again Li shook his head.

"Is this normal?" No answer. "Are you in pain?"

A shudder ran through the boy, his hand pausing momentarily. Once more the boy shook his head.

Malvern didn't believe him. How could the boy not be in pain looking the way he did?

Li straightened, his right hand tight around the rail. Defiant was what Malvern would have called it. Defiance the likes of which he hadn't seen since Hardstrom -

- who bellowed an order for the sails. The wind freshened, strong and steady, the kind *Cutty Sark* chased. He caught another order for a speed reading. "Seventeen and a half knots!" the sailor cried. Malvern could scarcely believe it. Even at best a clipper might be glad of fifteen knots, perhaps even sixteen.

He turned back to Li. He would have thanked him, but the race had only just begun. He raised the cup of tea to his lips and sipped. Fine tea. If he were first into London this would fetch an exorbitant price.

And the Angels Sang

☙❧

The following day they shot through Sunda Straight. *Thermopylae* long ago disappeared behind them.

Li still stood at the rail, impossibly, without food, without water, squatting like a woman when necessary over a slop bucket, that hand never ceasing its motion. The winds all but howled. Above, the sun hung white and hot in a sky so deeply blue you could fall into it.

Hardstrom danced across the deck, laughing, cajoling, his blue eyes the same wild color as the sky. "Get up there you salty knave," he shouted to the boy up the main. "Get up there and tell me what you see! Move that pretty arse!" The midshipman moved, higher and higher, speared to the sky.

"No sight of her, Sir!" the boy shouted back.

"No sight of her!" Hardstrom bellowed, laughing into the wind. "Count your shillings, you scurvy lot. We're for London and the highest price for tea!"

Malvern only watched from the forecastle, listening to the sounds of *Cutty Sark*. There had been another race like this. Malvern watched the scar on Hardstrom's face, a brand from the sea witch. Malvern watched Li's hand, relentless, restless.

It was then he lifted his nose and sniffed the wind. Aye, she was there. A gale. Far off, but a gale nonetheless.

His attention returned to Li. Was it his doing? Or was it the work of the Empress' minion? Reluctantly, Malvern asked himself was it possible the coming gale was the work of the sea witch herself, brewing the fulfillment of a bargain?

"Full sail, Hardstrom!" he bellowed.

"Full sail, aye, Captain!" he laughed, and the call ran up the masts, out the spars, over the lines.

Now it was a race against not only *Thermopylae* and the Empress Tz'u Hsi, but against the very winds that could kiss them or kill them.

☙❧

"Hurricane!" came the call from the nest, thin, torn on a wind already at gale force. "Hurricane a'comin'!"

Tempted as he was to fly before that mass of roiling black, Malvern gave the order to furl all but the jibs. As it was, one man nearly went overboard. *Cutty Sark's* decks were awash. Men scrambled like ghosts in a darkening sky.

"Get below," he bellowed to Li, who, despite all privations still stood at the rail. "Get below, you bastard, or you'll be overboard!"

Still the boy didn't move. Malvern yanked him from the rail. Li rounded on him, unbelievably his left hand still working the curve. Li snarled, ivory teeth in an ivory face.

"Get below!" Malvern roared.

In that moment the deck was awash, brine in his mouth, his belly on the deck and the air gone from his lungs. He reached through blindness, gasping, to grab the boy and haul him to safety. Somehow he found Li, caught him, dragged him across the listing deck, tumbled down the stairs to the main deck and when his breath and his vision returned, lashed him to the stairs. Still Li's hand moved, haltingly, hurtfully.

"Is this your doing?" he asked the boy.

Li answered nothing.

Malvern left him there. If he stayed he was sure he'd reshape the boy's face.

"Run before her!" he yelled at the struggling helmsman. "Hold her for your life!" And joined him at the wheel, his muscles pulling against the weight of an entire sea.

All but the storm jib shredded like paper. Through the rain Malvern could see men scrambling to cut the sails away, and then, while struggling with the wheel, Malvern saw Hardstrom out on the bowsprit, inching his way with a knife in his teeth and a grin on his face. In that moment the first mate seemed a wild creature defiant of the hurricane. A cliff of black water hung behind him. Whether it was his imagination or not he could swear he heard the sea-witch's laughter in the wind.

"Hardstrom!" Malvern yelled, desperate to bring the man back. "In the name of God, Hardstrom, come down!" but too late, too late, the wall gave way and smashed down on *Cutty Sark*.

When they emerged there was nothing left of either the sail or of Hardstrom. Still Malvern could hear Nanny's laughter through the wind.

"Curse you!" Malvern shouted, holding the wheel. His arms felt as if they'd pop from his shoulders. "Curse you, you whore of a sea!"

Lightning struck the mizzen. Light burst over the spars, jumping from line to line until the main and then the foremast blazed with St. Elmo's fire. In that moment of weird glory Li stood upon the bow of the boat, somehow untied, his hands raised to the heavens and he screamed a phrase to the wind.

With a lurch the wheel yanked at Malvern's arms. The helmsman was thrown from his side. The rudder was lost. He knew they were heading up onto the reefs around the Comoro Islands. *Cutty Sark's* hull would breach. Hardstrom, Hardstrom, gone in the wind.

Li's scream still echoed around him when they broke out of darkness onto a becalmed sea, a fiery sun setting in a cloudless sky.

☙❧

A pall settled over *Cutty Sark*. Not a breath of wind. Not a movement from the men. Only the sound of the sea slapped gently against the ship's sides. Brine dripped from spars moments ago engulfed in hurricane.

Where were they now? Certainly not in the eye of the storm, not with the sky perfectly clear all around them. Malvern yelled for Long the navigator. It took a moment but the man staggered toward him, his shoulder at an awkward twist.

"A bearing," he said after a moment.

Pain crossed Long's face, a careful breath drawn and let go. "I don't know, Captain. Nothing's right." He looked around the horizons. "Perhaps when the stars appear."

"Get yourself to the ship's surgeon."

Long managed a sketchy salute and staggered away.

"Second Mate Reeves," Malvern called, hoping he was still aboard. The man's "Aye-aye, Captain," answered him and within a moment the tall, blonde officer was in front of him, saluting. "I want a report of injuries, casualties and damage aboard ship."

"Right away, Sir." Reeves pivoted, bellowing orders to the crew who were still standing stunned and agape.

Malvern turned his gaze back to this placid world, in his mind seeing the way Hardstrom had been swept away, the memory of laughter in his ears.

He wheeled around to confront Li. When he came upon the foredeck Li was sprawled across the teak, that once luxuriant tunic torn and revealing what no gentleman should look upon. Unbelieving, Malvern could only stare at this male impersonator. Why hadn't he seen? It had been so obvious she impersonated a man. Fool that he was. Now he had a woman aboard his ship. Luck destroyed. Maybe all this had nothing to do with the sea witch. Maybe it had everything to do with the perils of having a female aboard a sailing ship.

"Surgeon!" he roared. "Get this woman off my deck!"

Li roused then, dragging herself upon her elbows and pulling the tatters of her tunic over her breasts.

"What have you done?" Malvern snarled.

For a Cup of Tea

She pushed her hair from her face. At that moment the ship's surgeon arrived. With a gesture she waved off any assistance and stood shakily, glaring defiantly at Malvern. "I brought us to a place of safety."

"And where might that be?" He would have given her a piece of his mind but that her eyes were brimming with tears.

"That's hard to say, exactly. We're safe. Repairs can be made."

"And then?"

"And then we return to the race."

"And you can do that?"

"Don't question my abilities."

"I'll question any bloody thing about you I wish, and I'd advise you to answer me directly if you wish me to remain a gentleman."

"Yes. I can return us to the race."

"Where we were?"

"Wherever I wish to put us." She turned on heel and stalked off toward her cabin.

"Damn you, girl, get back here!" She didn't.

&ash;

Keeping his crew calm while the new rudder was fashioned took delicacy and skill. Somehow Malvern managed to answer their questions. They seemed mollified.

Now, he lay in his bunk, rocked by a gentle sea albeit strange, desperately trying to make some sense of events. Sleep evaded him, exhausted though he was. He was just about to make his way on deck when a knock sounded delicately on his door.

He gave permission to enter. Li entered, bowed, hovered there in uncharacteristic uncertainty.

"What am I to call you now the impersonation is dispensed?" Malvern asked.

"I am the Lady May-ling Soong."

"I didn't think aristocratic ladies, especially decent aristocratic ladies, went around impersonating male prestidigitators."

"I was an impersonator of a man only."

"And not of a decent lady?"

"That's unfair."

"What's unfair is that you've landed me, my ship and my crew in a world I know nothing about. What's unfair is because of your bungling my first mate and best friend is now dead at sea. What's unfair is you've ruined every man aboard this ship should they ever return to England because every man

116

jack of them backed me in my wager." He rose from the bunk and crossed to her. "That's what's unfair."

"I can explain."

"I'm listening."

"The magician aboard *Thermopylae* is my brother, the Empress' lover."

"So?"

"He is what you might call an ambitious man. He was also my teacher. It's easier to risk a girl on untried knowledge, you see. No one questions the death of a girl in China."

He'd seen evidence of that kind of carelessness. "This explains the rivalry. It does nothing to explain why we're here."

"He deciphered my spell and twisted it. That's why I fought for so long, trying to regain control. When I couldn't, I did the only thing of which I could think – remove us from his influence."

"To where, exactly?"

"That I don't know." She looked away. "I was exhausted. There was so little time. I was trying to save Mr. Hardstrom." A tear tumbled down her cheek.

So the girl had some feeling. He offered her a handkerchief. "Can't you just enchant us back?"

She shook her head, her strain growing. "I need time."

"That isn't something of which we have a lot."

"I am aware."

"What would happen if you tried anyway?"

"I'd die. And you, your ship and your crew would likely be lost here."

"A lovely prospect." To take the harshness from his tone he smiled. Try as he might he found it difficult to curse her, not now he knew how expendable her life was to her brother and to those in China.

"I'm going above," he said thickly. "I'd suggest you remove yourself to your own cabin and rest. Our fate lies with you and your strength."

It was of that last pronouncement he thought when he came on deck to a silvery moon.

❧

The new rudder had been in place for several days. May-ling attempted to return them to the real world. All attempts were futile. At the moment she sat panting on the deck, trembling from the effort it had taken to cast that last spell.

"What seems to be the problem?" Malvern asked her.

"There's nothing to draw from."

"I don't understand."

She looked up at him, her face plainly expressing her pain. "When you ply the seas, you use the power around you, the power of wind, the power of rudder against water. If you have no wind you're left to drift in the current. What I do is similar. I draw from the spirit of water, from the spirit of wind."

He didn't like where this was leading. "So?"

"So there's nothing from which to draw here."

Malvern lowered his voice. "Are you saying we're marooned here?"

She looked away from him. "Perhaps."

He schooled his patience. "I need to understand. I'm responsible for all these men." For Hardstrom, for the death and pain he'd allowed because of a foolish wager.

Slowly, she looked back up to him. "There is only one spirit here and she dominates everything."

She. He wanted to ask, Is it her? Is it Nanny with whom you bargained? All he could say was, "And?"

"It would seem she's been bargained with one too many times. To keep the balance and free us of the storm, she took Mr. Hardstrom." Her voice broke then. "I didn't mean for it to happen that way."

Malvern closed his eyes, needing to hide and knowing he couldn't. "His life was forfeit anyway." As was his own. He'd bargained with Nanny as well. Checks and balances. Deftly kept. Now all sundered.

"I don't know what else to offer," she said. "I offered her myself and that's not good enough. I don't know what else to do."

Malvern knew. A captain always took responsibility for his crew.

❧

"I think I have an answer," May-ling said.

It was dawn of their fourth day marooned. To the east a band of cerulean blue topped a yellow glow, everything above that deep indigo. Not a single star shone, whether at dawn or deep of night. The navigator last evening assured Malvern they'd moved not at all.

The ship's surgeon made a test of sea water, to see if by boiling it they might stretch their supply. He'd died within moments of falling asleep. May-ling muttered something about the dream time.

Malvern was left no alternative now but to bargain directly with Nanny, his own life for that of his crew's. All the papers were in order. It could be done quite neatly now.

"What answer?" he asked May-ling, motioning her to a place removed from the men.

She tugged at the long braid over her shoulder. "There's another power source here I hadn't considered."

He motioned impatiently for her to continue.

"Another life," she said.

"You're not thinking of using the lives of my men?"

"Not the men, no," she answered.

"Then what, for the love of God?"

"The effreeti."

Her answer was as good as a plunge overboard. "What dangers are involved?"

"I have to gain control of it. That means it must be me who opens the jar. And it must be done on deck."

"I'd rather not have a bunch of mumbo jumbo up here to alarm the men."

"Do you know anything about effreeti?" she asked.

He indicated he didn't.

"They are wilful creatures, creatures of fire that live in magnificent brass cities on that elemental plane. Unless you wish this effreeti to set your ship ablaze, I'd suggest you allow me to release it up here. Effreeti are very large. They require room." She smiled tentatively. "And we want this effreeti to feel welcomed."

"Why?"

"Because if it doesn't feel welcomed after its long captivity, it may just decide to turn on all of us."

"And then?"

"And then I cajole and flatter it. They have rather enormous egos and it takes trickery and mastery to control one. Often they will attempt to do your bidding only to the letter of intent."

With some considerable trepidation, he asked, "And what of Nanny?"

May-ling arched a brow, plainly surprised he named the sea-witch. "She won't like it. I'll have to move quickly."

Bloody marvellous. "Do it."

※

The enormous brass bottle had been hauled above deck, the red wax carefully stripped and saved to one side. May-ling had the crew stand in a ring around the bottle, apparently as some form of greeting for the fire demon she'd release. Malvern couldn't help thinking that fire and water didn't mix.

At the moment May-ling spouted gibberish, drawing marks upon the deck around the bottle. A sense of panic was in her movements, a panic Malvern shared despite himself.

Just as he feared, the sea that had remained placid now grew restive. His hair blew about in a wind that had come up out of nowhere. His men shot uneasy glances at one another.

"Hurry, girl, hurry," he muttered under his breath, knowing it was a matter of time before they came face to face with Nanny.

May-ling turned her attention to the brass hinge on the jar. "Sing!" she shouted at the men. "Sing something to mollify her!"

They stood there gaping, unsure. Around them the wind howled. To his dismay Malvern saw how Nanny churned the sea, the circular path *Cutty Sark* took.

"Do as she says!" he ordered and struck up the first lines to a bawdy sea shanty extolling Nanny's virtues. May-ling struggled with the brass hinge. He tried to assist her only to be struck away.

"I have to open it," she hissed. "The effreeti follows whomever releases it."

About them the sky was a roiling mass, winds shrieking like the laughter of the witch. Around and around they spun. Malvern could do nothing but shout out the shanty, encourage his men to join him in a mad dance.

May-ling braced her feet upon the belly of the jar, shoving at the hinge.

"C'mon, girl, we're about to be bewitched!" he yelled, watching as a figure rose out of the nexus they circled. Huge Nanny was, dripping with kelp and crusted with barnacles, her gap-toothed mouth wide in a grimace Malvern could only assume was a greedy grin. Frantic now, he and his men danced for their very lives, singing praises of the sea-witch.

May-ling grunted, kicked. The bottle waggled, toppled. May-ling rolled over with the jar, yanking for all she was worth.

"Put your back into it, girl!" Malvern roared.

Nanny reached toward them, ponderous in her enormity. To his horror one of the crew was plucked from the deck like a flea from a shirt. Still May-ling hadn't uncorked that blasted effreeti. Malvern aimed his foot for May-ling's bottom and shoved just as she set her shoulder to the grip. She flipped end over end, the brass grip in her hands. Sailors went down like bottles bowled on the green. The stopper popped open. Nanny shrieked and dropped the sailor to the deck just as a giant creature of flame without heat emerged from the bottle and bowed to the Lady May-ling Soong.

"Free!" the creature roared, nearly shaking the ship to splinters.

"I remind you of honour," May-ling shouted.

Flickering wildly, the thing turned, surveying its surroundings. It looked at Nanny for a long moment and then turned back to May-ling. "What honour is there in a woman who deals with water things?"

"I do not deal with her. I deal only with great and noble spirits, spirits who understand the meaning of honour."

The effreeti considered this while Malvern shouted for a little more alacrity. Nanny screamed and screamed, reached now for Malvern himself. His life was forfeit, he knew.

"Will you serve me?" May-ling asked. "As only your noble kind may."

"For one hundred and fifteen days I will serve you."

Malvern felt as if the ocean itself closed over him when Nanny clutched him into her hand.

May-ling shouted, "Take this ship, this crew and myself to London, England."

"As you wish."

Malvern gasped, sucking in air, real air. He was about to yell at May-ling to instruct the effreeti to take them to London ahead of *Thermopylae*, only to find himself aboard *Cutty Sark*, yes, but anchored near the Thames docks. Belatedly he thought he ought to have also asked her to have the fire demon deal with the sea-witch.

His head felt detached. His knees he was sure had been replaced by jelly. Around him he could hear the cheers of his crew. An upstart of a lad bellowed from a cutter to have the captain repair ashore. The boy didn't seem at all ruffled by the fact they'd just popped into harbour.

"What day is it, lad?" Malvern yelled, gripping the rail firmly lest he find himself flat on his rump.

"Why, it's Tuesday, sir."

"And the date?"

"March 17, 1872."

March 17! One hundred and four days from Shanghai to London! "Has *Thermopylae* anchored?"

"No, sir. May I tell the harbour master you're coming, Sir?"

"Aye! Indeed!" He laughed. "Bring us ashore, men, bring us ashore!"

❧

Three days later *Thermopylae* sailed into port, her captain 1,000 British pounds lighter and her cargo to fetch a price that would likely set Brown back apiece. Malvern would have gloated over his win but for the packet he'd sent to Hardstrom's mother. Perhaps it was to pay his respect to Hardstrom, or perhaps it was to ease his conscience, whatever the reason he'd included his own commission as well as Hardstrom's share. The remainder had been divided equally among his men.

At the moment he stood ashore, watching *Cutty Sark's* cargo being unloaded. May-ling stood next to him, fresh from having delivered the empty but sealed bottle to the London Museum. Her brother, apparently, flew into a rage and boarded a ship leaving for the Americas that very day, fleeing the wrath of the Empress.

"There's been little time to speak with you," May-ling said, "and I wanted to thank you, Captain."

He grunted a reply. He was about to do the courteous thing and ask her what she would be doing, when a shipping agent strode toward him, asking for Captain Robertson Giles Malvern.

"I'm he," Malvern said. "What may I do for you?"

"Ah, Captain Malvern," the man said, extending a hand. "Mr. Brinkman, representing Fartham's Textiles. I was wondering if you'd be interested in a run to Melbourne for the wool trade. We'd be willing to pay a premium to have you sail – "

"We'll do it," May-ling answered. "Four pounds per ton – "

"Now just a moment," Malvern said, rounding on her. "I'll not have you meddling – "

"I'm sure you can settle the rest of the arrangements," she said, turned and sauntered up the boarding ramp to *Cutty Sark*, the flame-like effreeti appearing and floating at her back.

"Come back here!"

"Are you agreed then?" Brinkman asked.

Four pounds per ton! Extravagant! "Aye, agreed," Malvern barked and charged up the ramp after May-ling. "Get back here you witch!"

Figure 15: Pen & ink sketch, Marika Rozins

Summer Wine and Sweet Mistresses
Previously published, The Blotter, 1986

A summer breeze played around Willis, his thin lips puckering in a smile. He paused, lifting away the sweat under his cap with his arm, his other arm against the old oak. From the time he was a boy, people had been accustomed to seeing him tending the trees, and in some respects he'd become a part of the trees; to park rangers and regular visitors Willis was a familiar, the old man of the trees, as they'd come to call him.

But Willis' time was coming to an end. That was why Jason – somewhere in the limbs overhead – was learning all the old man had to teach.

"Hey, Jas," Willis called, his neck arching to give him a better view of the young man. The branches bobbed.

"Yeah! What now?"

Willis grinned, his colourless eyes sparkling. "Be nice to her. Be nice to her and she'll be nice back."

"It's just a tree." Jason leapt from his perch. He rolled when he hit the ground, his arches smarting. "Jesus! Must have been higher than I thought."

Willis' hand remained on the belly of the oak. "You offended her, that's all."

Jason glared at the old man, exasperated with all the mystic, lorish garbage he'd been fed since beginning this job. The old man wouldn't even let him apply his university education – made some speech about no need for chemicals and nonsense here. The trees of this park were tended with love.

Love! More nonsense about dryads and intelligent plants. If the old man didn't let him use chemicals that oak he raved about would die within the year.

Roughly, Jason hauled himself to his feet. "I'll judge my distance carefully next time."

Willis was still grinning, his hand still upon the tree. He nodded as if someone had said something profound, and then: "Whad'd they teach you in that agriculture school?"

"Lots I could teach you."

"That so? And I'm tellin' ya, boy, if ya don't harken, me and the oak'll die 'cause of your bumbling."

"Very funny."

Willis' grin vanished. "I'm dead serious, boy. They don't call me the old man of the trees fer nothin', y'know."

Anger darkened Jason's face, his hands knotting around his kit and tools. "Damn you! If you'd let me tend the oak like I know how, it'll be here long after both you and I are gone."

"Ya like larnin' boy, don't ya."

Jason shrugged. "Sure. I wouldn't have wasted my time in university otherwise."

"Well, I'm about ta larn ya somethin'." He shifted his weight to the other foot, one hand still upon the tree, the other beckoning to Jason. "C'mere and listen to her heart."

Jason sniggered, his head shaking. "I think you've fallen from one too many trees."

"C'mere and do as I say!"

The tools and kit slipped from his hands as he advanced to Willis, nervousness ticking along his temples.

"Tha's right," Willis said. "Now lay yer hand along side mine. Gentle now, tha's my mistress you're caressin'."

"She good?"

"Be civil. She's always been a lady."

"Christ! You talk like she's alive."

Willis frowned. "She eats, drinks and breathes, don't she?"

Perhaps Jason had pushed the old man a little too far. He set his hand beside Willis'.

The bark beneath his palm was warm, leathery the way he imagined an old woman's nipple might be, and he assumed the heat to have been from sunlight. When he turned his head over-shoulder, panic hit him. This side of the tree remained in shadow all day and should have been cool. He checked the bark for moss and lichen. There were radiant green patches mottling the area around his hand, no signs of sunburn or dryness... and yet the bark was palpably warm.

It was then a shudder swept through the tree, engulfing him. To Jason it seemed as if the tree throbbed beneath his fingers.

In the next moment he found himself on the grass, his head between his knees. All he could hear was ringing in his ears, as if he'd fainted.

"Damn!" he said. "I must've hit my head in that fall."

Willis' boots were planted before his line of sight. Jason looked up to that craggy face.

"No concussion, boy. Just the beat of her heart." There was no arguing when Willis stalked away.

For the remainder of the day Jason drowned in a sea of confusion, the weird occurrence haunting him; he avoided the old oak, pressing his skills upon the other trees. His obsession to avoid the oak and Willis consumed him so that he found himself working well past quitting time. Still, the oak dominated his thoughts. Exhausted and raw with apprehension, he finally returned to the scene of that afternoon occurrence and flung himself upon the grass.

Before him the matronly oak grew astride the crest of a hill, overlooking the expansive park. It was a tranquil scene, like sitting upon the throne of the world. Now more than ever the oak seemed like an empress.

Off to the west the sun liquefied the horizon, so that at the height of the dome it was indigo, then magenta, then orange, then gold – royal colours for a royal dominion. There was nothing to mar that perfect scene: brilliant sky, cool forest, solitary hill.

An evening breeze stirred the leaves. That seemed like a seduction to rest.

A mistress ...

Again the memory of that warmth tingled his palm. Despite himself Jason smiled. He accepted the invitation and stretched among the roots of the oak, his arms beneath his head. For awhile he studied the tricks of sunset on the leaves, the green-gold transparencies and dark, cool under-leaves. Stars of sunlight bounced over his head, soft sensuous rustling lulling his turmoil. Like a musky perfume the oak's smell entangled his senses, leaving him adrift in a universe of sensation; green-gold lights and dark leaves, cool grass and warm sun, pungent earth and clean air. Even the taste on his tongue was bittersweet, like the after-bite of a cool, summer wine.

Summer wine and a sweet mistress ...

He was distantly aware of his muscles unclenching, of the long, deep rhythms of his breathing. He knew that he was falling asleep, alone, in a vast parkland, and that night would come crashing down in a matter of minutes, but despite all his inner warnings he remained stretched out at the foot of the oak.

Just when he actually slept, Jason was unsure ... if indeed he slept at all. Night swept around him. Above him the stars had flung a reckless welcome, and on the horizon a luminous balloon drifted into spectacle. The moon seemed read to merge with the earth, filling the lower half of the sky. Its light was so bright there were shadows on the grass. That was when Jason flinched.

Shadows.

A long slender darkness rippled across the ground at his feet, at its source a woman clad in shades of night and fragrance. When she moved it was like the rustle of the leaves. When she breathed it was like the intoxication of the earth. When she gazed on him it was like the warmth of the oak. Everything about her was dark, earthy, sweet. Her hair was dark, shifting about her calves. Her limbs were dark like the smooth roundness of new branches. Her eyes were dark like the secret shadows of evening leaves. His caution itched but he refused to scratch. He sat up and tried to speak. As if suddenly mute he found himself incapable of speech. But that didn't seem to ruffle the moonlight lady. She drifted toward him, rippling down beside him and kissed his mute mouth. Wave after wave of sweet summer wine washed across his lips.

Summer wine and a sweet mistress ...

The rest of her caresses exploded into dreams.

When Jason woke, the sun was already pitched toward the west. He sprang upright and groaned. A blinding pain engulfed sight and sound. His head cleared in a moment, but his confusion swelled to gross proportions: Willis sat cross-legged on the ground beside him, that unnerving grin brightening that ruddy complexion.

"Slept a little, eh?"

Jason ran his hand through his hair. "I got carried away and fell asleep ..."

"Carried away! She's quite the gal, my old oak."

Jason was aware of the distant ashes of passion. He felt grey. "She'll die if you don't let me work on her."

Willis chuckled. "Work on her? Oh, I don't think that matters now."

He could do little but glare at the old man, and feeling crusty, he stalked off to the staff grounds to shower, eat and fling himself into study.

When the evening again stained the day, his escape was again cut short. Willis let himself into the cabin without invitation and stood extending a ring of wood to Jason. The old man seemed placid ... somehow younger.

"Me'n the old gal would like ya ta have this, Jas."

"What is it?" He swivelled away from the desk.

"A gift given to me when I first started on here. The guy I replaced gave it ta me, and I guess you could say I'm kinda carryin' on th' tradition." He made a gesture with his open palm. "Go ahead. Take it."

Jason remained where he was. "I thought I was being hired as your assistant, not your replacement."

"I'm getting' kinda old ta be ramblin' 'round here."

Jason pushed himself out of the chair and accepted the ring.

"Belongs on yur left hand ... third finger."

"Like a wedding band."

"Could say that." Willis shrugged. "I'll be a'goin' now. Jus gonna say g'bye to the old gal."

Dread and joy swept over Jason. The smooth oak ring lay in the palm of his hand. It looked old, ancient, stained with the sweat of many hands. The edges were round and shiny.

Truth smacked him like a blow. He flinched. He jammed the circle of oak into his plaid pocket, flung open the door and sprinted for the hill that dominated the landscape.

By now night robbed the day of colour and left only a monochrome dimension to his surroundings. The same giant golden ball was rising behind the oak. Jason knew he would be too late. But still he ran.

When he came to the foot of the hill he collided with futility. Above him spread the silhouette of the gnarled oak and stooped old man beneath it. The oak trembled. Its trunk bulged against the moonlight. Within seconds, although it seemed like an eternity to Jason, the bulge separated into a slim, fluid figure, one he knew from what he thought was a dream.

A mistress ...

If he had thought to be romantic he might have found the scene of the woman and Willis a touching one. But Jason was numb. Everything he knew, had studied and understood, evaporated into moonlight. The oak stood dark and mysterious against the moon, Willis no longer there.

Slowly, he crept up the hill, his heart beating with a new emotion. When he came beside the tree he caressed the bark as if he were caressing a lover. A shiver ran over him. He smiled. And then he slipped the ring on his finger and lay beneath the fragrant boughs.

Figure 16: Digital painting, Lorina Stephens

Dragonslayer

While the messenger from the Regional Taxation Office cooled his heels over a cuppa with Mrs. Braunswagger - none other than the legendary elven princess, Starwithen - Simon Braunswagger - otherwise known from the war as Dragonslayer - continued to ply his trade as a life insurance salesman.

At the moment he was in the kitchen of Mrs. Boghill, some distance north in the village of Hog's Hollow, under the shadow of Mount Ummer. To be accurate he was flat on his back on Mrs. Boghill's kitchen table, addressing her needs. Which, it would seem were considerable. The fact this lady of varied charms was halfling was of no consequence to Simon. All the ladies were pleased when he came to call. Passionate, one might say. In fact, eager. It was a question of size, you see. Human men - well, they were so much better proportioned than halfling.

"I'm sure you can see the benefits of insuring your husband's life," Simon said. He grinned at his reflection in the large silver tray on the sideboard to his left, supine though he was. Mrs. Boghill shifted over him. He watched her hike her petticoats a little higher.

"Oh yes, yes," Mrs. Boghill said a little breathlessly. "Mmm ... sizable benefits. I'm willing to do anything you think advisable."

It made a delightful scene in that tray, Mrs. Boghill eager to negotiate. The table creaked in protest. He reached down to his leather satchel, pulling out a contract. She shifted slightly. A willing client indeed. The contract fell from his hand.

"A very wise decision," he replied. He offered a value-added contract. Mrs. Boghill clapped her hands over her mouth in her excitement, which was just as well. He didn't want that brat in the bedroom to awaken, not at least until he had his bonus, which came, in a manner of speaking, in the rush of the next few moments. Mrs. Boghill moaned her agreement to the terms.

Alert to the sale, Simon set Mrs. Boghill on the table beside him.

"Mr. Boghill will be home for tea in a few moments," she giggled. "He can sign the papers then."

And the Angels Sang

Simon slapped her bottom as she scampered off the table. He fluffed the ruffles at his throat when Mr. Boghill stumped through the kitchen door, shot a glance at the missus, who was at the hearth, and then at Simon.

"Who'sat?" Boghill asked, hooking a thumb in Simon's direction.

"Why, darling, this is Mr. Braunswagger from the Mid-realm Life Assurance Company." Mrs. Boghill set the teapot beside cups and saucers on the table. Steam curled from the spout of the brown pot.

Simon bent and extended his hand to the burly halfling. "I understand you served in the war, Sir."

Boghill sputtered, shook Simon's hand. "I did indeed. Why, 'tis a pleasure to be meeting you, Mr. Braunswagger, or should I be calling you Mr. Dragonslayer?"

"It's not dragons I'm conquering these days."

Boghill plunked down into one of the diminutive chairs. "It's a sorry state we're in now the war's over." He nodded in the general direction of Mount Ummer. "Even that dragon up yonder's not worth worrying about."

"They confiscated her hoard of brimstone?"

"Oh, aye. Took it from her feeding place while she was napping on the mound."

"A sorry state indeed." Simon accepted a cuppa from Mrs. Boghill. "You ever thought of life insurance?"

"Life insurance is it then?" Boghill slurped tea from his saucer. "Well that's a thing most of us should have thought of before the war, I say." He leaned conspiratorially toward Simon. "I'll lay you odds most o' them young'uns these here widows have are the product of some ill-begotten war relations."

"Or some ill-begotten marital relations," Mrs. Boghill put in.

Simon smiled, inching the contract in front of Boghill. "What I'm offering you is pride, Mr. Boghill. There'll be no welfare for your sweet wife when you pass away. No, sir. You'll have taken care of your obligations."

"Lovey, 'tis a grand idea," Mrs. Boghill said, bending near her husband to display her ample pleasure. Boghill swallowed hard and turned back to Simon.

"Oh, aye. 'Tis a grand idea. But what's this to cost a poor man?"

"A mere pittance," Simon said, flourishing a quill and an inkpot. "You won't even notice." He offered the quill to Boghill, who looked at his wife, then over to Simon. Boghill scratched his X in the eighteen appropriate places and Simon was out the door, calculating his commission. It wouldn't go far. Perhaps he should give some consideration to trading contraband goods. He had enough contacts. Just last week Bertrand from Vale Harbour sent a letter by private courier, saying he needed a man of Simon's skills.

131

Seems they were running all manner of contraband. Just the sort of adventuring he liked.

He'd reply within the week, he decided.

Dusk hovered over the violet hills when finally he clopped up his lane on his faithful steed, mist gathering in the vale. His cottage wasn't as yet visible, hidden by a screen of golden linden trees Starwithen insisted on transplanting from her elven forest. Wood-smoke was on the chill autumn air, a warm smell he would have welcomed were it not for the fact there would likely again be a rabbit stew in the pot. No venison for him. Not like in the old days.

Selling life insurance had been fine those first few years after the war. There was no mercenary work, and selling life insurance hadn't been too different to military strategy. What really made it worthwhile in those early days was the halflings of the island had been eager, the memory of lost loved ones fresh.

His problem now was the little buggers were so damned long-lived. There were probably only a handful of new clients left. The next generation hadn't matured enough yet to bring him any new commissions. In the interim his pocket suffered and the company hounded him about declining sales.

Not for the first time he wished his renown as a brilliant swordsman brought him more than awe among the locals. Being wonderful had its drawbacks.

More and more Bertrand's offer had its merits. Sugar was hard to find, and the halflings had more than a liking for it. Tobacco was even rarer. Last time he'd seen Bertrand the man had puffed a pipeful that would have had these halflings on their knees.

He cast a glance over-shoulder in the direction of Mount Ummer.

And what about brimstone? Just a little. Just enough to let the old girl up there keep her dignity.

Come to think of it, running contraband couldn't be that much different from selling life insurance, or soldiering.

When he rounded the linden he reined in, letting his hand glide over the steed's neck to settle its propensity to bolt. "What's this?" he murmured.

Hobbled in his front garden was a palomino pony, fatter than a regular riding animal should have been, and considerably shaggier. That could only mean its owner knew little about mounts. Most likely a halfling or dwarf, although the latter seemed unlikely. There hadn't been dwarves in these parts since before the war.

Simon's attention lingered on the saddlebags that were tooled of rich leather, the official crest of the region stamped upon each. He looked to the row of windows at the front of the cottage, cursing the extravagant lace

And the Angels Sang

Starwithin had imported. Little was visible through the lace, certainly no movement. Candles, however, blazed with Starwithen's usual disregard for frugality.

This could only mean trouble, he was sure.

Cautious, he nudged his steed toward the stable, dismounted, unsaddled and left currying until oats had appeased the animal's disposition, and he'd found out what this visitor meant.

Simon listened through the open half of the back door. Beneath the regular bickering of his four adolescents, Simon heard the rise and fall of two voices – that sweet melodic voice could only be Starwithen's. The other was unfamiliar. There was a drawl to the voice, every word meandering around a profligate amount of ems and ums. Simon groaned. That voice could only mean one thing – a government official.

What, in the name of all hells, could the government want with him? He'd been careful to hide any tax fraud. Those halflings in government couldn't have been smart enough to find him out.

An audit?

Maybe this visit had to do with Starwithin? Was it possible? Surely not. She was only an elven princess, one of the last to remain after the Great War. What was she before his fame, his legend, his infinite prowess?

That was when he thought of Bertrand and the letter in his satchel.

He unlatched the lower door and stepped into the kitchen, looking in the brass tea tray on the table to be sure his hair was tidy, his smile blinding, his jaw unshadowed. Damn, but he was a perfect specimen of masculine flesh. He grinned at himself, flashing enamel.

At that moment Starwithin came in to retrieve the tea service. Abruptly, Simon straightened. His curiosity completely mastered him when she scowled, her double chin wobbling.

"Get yourself into the parlour," she said, clearly forgetting who was master in this cottage. "There's a messenger from the Regional Taxation Office here to see you, and if you shut-up long enough, and manage to keep even an ounce of that air between your ears attentive, there might be a job in it for you." She snatched up the tea service. "And in the name of all magic, don't slouch!"

Well, at least an audit or charges of tax fraud weren't in question.

Simon sighed as he watched Starwithin retreat into the parlour, his attention on her wide bottom. Whatever had gotten into the wench? Letting her lack of respect slide for the moment, he entered the parlour, putting on his best smile.

In the large chair by the hearth sat a toad of a halfling, his red velvet coat and breeches dusty from the road. In his arms he clasped a leather satchel.

Simon made note of the dirty footprints staining that hellishly expensive silk rug.

"Mr. Braunswagger, I assume," the halfling said, pre-empting Starwithin's introduction. "I'm Mr. Woolriven, from the Regional Taxation Office." He extended a hairy hand.

Simon crossed to a table under the window where a series of crystal decanters glittered in the candlelight, chose one with an amber brandy and poured himself a tumbler full. Mr. Woolriven looked on hopefully, which then became disbelief when Simon made no offer.

"Do be polite," Starwithin said, fixing Simon with one of her best withering stares.

"I am, dumpling." He glared at her, turned back to the halfling. "What do you want?"

Quickly, the halfling closed his gaping mouth and reached into the satchel.

"I don't want paperwork," Simon said after a mouthful of brandy. That brought the halfling's head up. "I want to know why you're here."

"Well, yes, Mr. Braunswagger - "

"Dragonslayer to you."

"Perhaps if you just came to the point," Starwithin said, "it might ease my husband's apprehension."

The halfling reached deeper into the satchel. "Well, yes, Mr. Dragonslayer, if you'd just let me - "

"You've a brain don't you?" Simon said.

"Yes, Mr. - "

"Then surely you don't need some document to tell you why you've come here?" Starwithin's look would have fried Simon on the spot, he was sure.

"Well, no, but procedure dictates - "

"Screw procedure."

"Simon, really!" Starwithin shrieked.

"Shut it! What the hell do you want, Woolriven?"

Starwithin's cup clattered on her saucer, her mouth opening to rain down a storm of reprimands. Simon waved off her protests. Apparently completely surprised, Starwithin closed her mouth. She only sat there staring at her husband with growing incomprehension.

The halfling gulped, his hand retreating from the satchel. "Taxation's having difficulty collecting the treasury tax from Elmagradon on Mount Ummer."

Simon laughed. "You're taxing dragons?"

"Well, yes - "

"Then you've no brains.

"They're totally harmless now we've put government controls on brimstone."

He crossed to the chair and leaned over the halfling, an action that clearly left the wee man in a state of alarm. "You ever been near a dragon?"

"Well, no – "

"Then you know shit about what dragons can and can't do."

"Simon, watch your language," Starwithin said.

"And I said stow it!"

"Simon, what Mr. Woolriven is about to offer you could be – "

"Could be what? Lucrative? Did you spend something you shouldn't, my princess? I've had an exhausting day. If you'd kindly mind your place, wench, then I'd be able to ascertain just what, exactly, this excuse for a halfling is about."

Starwithin raised the cup in her hand, aiming it, to which Simon answered, "Do that, my pretty, and I'll find some way of showing my gratitude."

Her face blanched, her hand lowering.

Mr. Woolriven closed his eyes, clasped his trembling hands together. "It may be we know little about dragons, Mr. Dragonslayer, but we need your help."

"My help?" Again Simon laughed. "To collect your tax? Piss off." He wondered what kind of pay Taxation might offer, how much of the haul he might be able to extort.

"You're our last hope!"

Simon turned his back and strode to the window where darkness gathered at the casement. The first stars glimmered. He thought again of camp at the end of a day's journey, of a fire snapping, of stars encrusting the heavens. There would have been bawdy songs sung by fighting men, and bawdy nights tucked up with willing wenches.

But now. Now you couldn't trust anything. The wenches all had notions of liberation. All the fighting men were dead or sold door to door as he. Taxes were opprobrious. Food expensive. His own four brats shouted from upstairs. He winced.

What he couldn't do now was let Woolriven know he'd sell Starwithin and his life as an insurance salesman to have one last go at a dragon.

"What, exactly, were you hoping I'd do?" he asked.

He heard Woolriven let go of a breath, heard Starwithin sigh.

"We were hoping you'd go up Mount Ummer and convince Elmagradon it would be in her best interest to pay the treasure tax."

"Let's not belabour the obvious. What else?"

"And if she refuses you'll slay her and collect the tax anyway."

"That's quite an incentive for her to pay. Tell me, does the Taxation Office treat all citizens in this manner?"

"Well, no - "

"Then why treat dragons like this?"

"Well, she is after all only a dragon."

Simon whirled, feigning anger. "Only a dragon? And what, pray tell, might you only be?" He scowled. "Only a halfling, and not much of a one at that. Tell me, why am I your last hope?"

"We've exhausted all other means - "

"Which translated means, how many others have died?"

The halfling looked down at his satchel. "Six."

"Six. My, you are an efficient bunch. And how many of those were fighters?"

"Three."

That wounded. He couldn't help but wonder who were the other three they chose before him? Wasn't he legendary? Wasn't he magnificent? "What's in it for me?"

Woolriven looked up. "A ten percent commission - "

"Make it fifty."

"Twenty-five."

Hah! "Thirty."

"A thirty percent commission, agreed."

"And expenses there and back, as well as compensation for sales commissions I would have lost while cleaning up for you."

"Really, Mr. - "

"Take it or leave it."

"We'll take it." Woolriven shook his head. "You drive a hard bargain."

"You want me, those are my terms."

"How soon can you begin?"

"Three days."

The halfling sighed in relief. He handed Simon that odious sheaf of documents he'd been keeping in the satchel. "This will tell you exactly what we're looking for. There are also documents you will have to have Elmagradon sign, as well as waivers for you to sign."

Simon riffled the sheaf. "Waivers?"

"To state your heirs and assigns will make no claim against the government should you - "

"Don't you dare sign anything like that!" Starwithin warned.

"For once, sweetling, I agree with you."

"I don't know," Woolriven said. "This is highly irregular."

"If I was a regular sort of fighter you wouldn't be coming to me." Not that he needed to worry about the waiver. He hadn't won the title of Dragonslayer by being incompetent.

"I'll see what I can do," Woolriven said, and slid off the chair.

Starwithin saw the halfling to the door. Simon turned back to the window where the sky was a river of stars, thinking this might be the first moment of a new career. When Starwithin announced dinner, there was rabbit stew.

༄༅

He sent a letter to Bertrand immediately after that idiot halfling left. Within two days he had his reply. After that he'd set out armoured and resplendent, amid cheers, through the village and onto the road that wound through heavily pined hills at the base of Ummer. Once free of the forest, he maintained a course up the craggy slopes that was visible to the villages below. They'd be composing songs about him before he even made it home – Simon Braunswagger. Dragonslayer. The Legendary. The Magnificent.

He thought of Starwithin's hands. Her farewell to him had been sweaty and sweet, as had Mrs. Boghill's and most of the ladies he'd stopped to see along the way. With women absolutely the last thing on his mind, he felt free to plan his line of attack.

When his course took him out of sight of the villages below, he shed his armour. This was, perhaps, a little foolhardy. But he trusted his instincts with dragons. It had been ten years since the war, three during – enough time for Elmagradon to have laid and incubated the clutch he was sure she carried when last he'd seen her. A new mother, without support, was just the kind of quarry he understood.

For the next ten days he rode through brilliant sun and blinding rain, slain a bear in a cave where he took shelter and generally had himself a jolly time.

This morning, Simon leaned over the horn of his saddle, studying the path that led to the infamous cave of Mount Ummer. His shadow stretched out before him.

A profusion of carcasses and bones littered the stone before Elmagradon's lair, some animal, some halfling, others plainly human. The most recent fighter sprawled not a bowshot away, her head a dessert for vultures, her torso, some few feet farther, clearly gnawed by a dragon. No doubt Elmagradon was allowing this latest kill to ripen a bit before dining – easier for dragonets that way.

It had been some years since he'd smelled dragon. The reality of it was every bit as pungent as the memory. Gagging, he loosened his satchel from the packhorse, checked the inkpot, and, satisfied he was as well equipped as he'd ever be, called out to the lady of the cave.

There was nothing visible in that maw of darkness. A grunt was all he received as reply. He turned back to the packhorse and untied a huge hunk of bear from the sledge. With some considerable effort – it was amazing how out shape he'd become – he dragged the meat into the entrance just short of the bones. He withdrew a cautious distance.

"Ms. Elmagradon, perhaps you remember me? We met briefly when you slew that band of orcs in the raid on Meipi? Simon Braunswagger?"

There was definite shuffling, the clink of gold coins, sniffing. "The one they call Dragonslayer?"

"Well, yes, ma'am, but they were evil dragons, not the law-abiding type like yourself."

"What is it you want?"

"I was wondering if you'd allow me to pay my respects to your new clutch?"

"What would a dragon-murdering piece of shit like you want to do that for?"

"As I said before, I only slay evil dragons. And as for paying my respects – well, it's just the proper thing to do."

In the darkness two eyes were now visible.

"You're naked."

Simon smiled. "I assure you I'm not."

"Then where's that carapace you always wear?"

"Why would I need armour?"

There was a rumble and then: "So peace has brought you to this."

"Deplorable, I know, to see a man of my skills reduced to civilian life. May I come in?"

She grunted assent. With a bow, Simon entered, careful to step over the bones strewn about the entrance. He knew enough about dragons to respect their art of bone collage.

Carefully, he reached to her golden scales and stroked her long neck, relishing the satiny warmth of dragon skin. She was thinner than he remembered, the ridges along her back prominent. In response, she purred and made mention of how long it had been since she'd had a good back scratch.

Ever willing to gain her confidence, he stripped off his boots and clambered up her back, rubbing his hands over her scales. To scratch a dragon's back is no small task and so it was some hours before she finally had her fill and took Simon deeper into the cave to show off her dragonets.

There were only two of them, twenty feet long a piece, the dull bronze color of young dragons. Behind them glittered a hoard of treasure that would have made a weaker man drool.

He was about to compliment her on her family when one of the dragonets opened its mouth in an attempt to spew out fire, which, of course, came to nothing more than a foul burp without brimstone to brew in its belly.

This gave him the edge he'd been looking for. "I'll be frank with you, Ms. Elmagradon." That enormous head turned toward him. It occurred to Simon he'd simply be an appetizer to her, a small but oh so succulent morsel. "The Taxation department sent me."

Her eyes narrowed, her jaw opening.

"But perhaps you and I can work something out that will be mutually beneficial, and still keep Taxation out of your life."

Her jaw closed. "Such as?"

"What if you were to pay the tax?"

"The others all had the same idea."

"Not quite. Hear me out. Let's just say you pay the tax."

"Okay, and deny my children their heritage? The full hoard?"

"What if the hoard could be recuperated?"

"I'm listening."

"What if you were to take out a life insurance policy on yourself, payable for the amount Taxation's about to dun you, with beneficiaries your two dragonets?"

"I don't get it."

"No. But they will." He nodded to the dragonets. "You see, when you die in the far distant future, your children will reap the benefits you have sown for them. The policy will pay them an amount equal to what went missing because of the taxes. And further, we could tie the policy to some excellent investments to make that amount grow, so your family will, in fact, inherit a sizeable sum beyond what you invested."

"And what good will that do them when they're dragons without power?"

"Ah, the brimstone."

"Yes, the cursed brimstone. I can't even teach them one of the essential things of being a dragon."

"Well, that is a problem, but I'm sure I can work something out."

"Not with those officious asses."

"Who was saying anything about officious asses?"

"And just how are you going to get your hands on brimstone if I can't?"

"I still have contacts, favours to call. There's a very good possibility I could lay my hands on brimstone, not a lot, but enough for, say, cultural purposes. Of course, there would be some risk, and considerable cost to me - "

Her eyes gleamed. "I'll pay whatever costs. If you can supply me with brimstone for the young ones, I'll pay the tax, keep the government happy –"

"Not draw any attention."

"Exactly."

He smiled and told her to wait but a moment, turned and retrieved the back-bending lumpy sack from the packhorse. Elmagradon already twitched with anticipation when he came back. Clearly there was nothing wrong with her nose.

With a grin, he dumped out the contents of the sack. Yellow, powdery rocks scattered across the stone.

"I believe this should be enough for your dragonets."

She snorted with excitement.

"But you'll have to promise you'll not consume any yourself. If word were to get out that the dragon on the mount were breathing fire – "

"They'd send an army after me."

He nodded.

She sighed, looking with longing at the pile of yellow stone.

"But at least what it means to be a dragon won't be lost," he offered.

"True." She turned her head to the young ones who were sniffing the yellow brimstone, nuzzled one of them. "How much will this cost?"

"A pittance. A mere pittance, most glorious Elmagradon. Shall we say a sack for a sack?"

She glanced at her hoard, back to the sack, clearly measuring just how much of that pile would disappear. Finally: "Seems fair."

Which was just what he knew she'd say. He wasn't asking a lot, not by comparison to what had accumulated on that mound.

With great care, suitable praise for her mighty dragonness, Simon took himself and several sacks around the family and began loading a lifetime of wealth. Once the taxes had been loaded, he took care of his share. In his rummaging he found a mirror, nothing that looked too magical, but it did give a perfect reflection of himself, which, in the end, was the best magic of all. It went into the sack.

The rest of what he loaded was mostly in coin, substance that was easy to hide and wouldn't draw notice. Wouldn't do to have Starwithin thinking they were filthy rich. She'd be off on a shopping orgy before he could finish his nuptial duties.

He returned to Elmagradon and retrieved his satchel. By now the dragonets had ingested a small portion of the brimstone and were belching.

Elmagradon was saying, "No, from the diaphragm. Breathe, swallow air, hold it," which they did, "a little longer," their mouths puffed out, "now exhale." Yellow flame blazed right into the face of their mother. She bellowed. They ducked their heads. She laughed that barking, ear-shattering laugh of a dragon. "Such darlings!"

They pranced. They preened. A perfect opportunity.

"About that life insurance, most magnificent one," Simon said.

"Ah yes. I'll be wanting a life insurance policy. Have to think of the future, you know."

He grinned. "I am awed by your acumen, Ms. Elmagradon. I would never have thought of that myself." He pulled contracts and documents from his satchel. He'd be sure to dispatch a letter to Bertrand tomorrow. It seemed his career had taken a prosperous turn. Life insurance and contraband just might be ideal complements. "If I may have your dragonprint? – here, that's it, and here, and here. Legal papers, you know how they are. Just a few more."

Figure 17: Watercolour and pen & ink painting, Lorina Stephens

Smile of the Goddess

Published previously, Sword & Sorceress X, ed. Marion Zimmer Bradley

She watched him ride under the dark of the moon, his generals beside him, an army at his back. He paused at the crest of the hill. Before him lay a pan of dried salt – the remnant of a sea she remembered retreating millennia ago – beyond that a dark rise that was the city of Nahrain of the kingdom of Oduman. Barad's kingdom.

A desert wind chilled his face. The bay under him snorted.

Consider, Barad, she said to him.

He touched his ear, raising his gaze to a river of stars. The beard he'd taken to did nothing to soften his face. Such a hard face, a fierce face. She heard him form her name, *Seditha?* Wondering, hoping he had indeed received the blessing of the goddess.

I can give you what you asked.

An image of his supplication in her temple filled his mind – the goat he'd sacrificed, the golden platters of dates, nuts and oranges, the way he'd prostrated himself before her priestess. King Barad on his belly. King Barad who had conquered a desert, who had liberated a people, who had forged peace when it seemed none could be achieved, tenuous though that peace might be.

King Barad had once again come to the goddess Seditha to ask her blessing upon a political mission.

Again she questioned his need: *Are you sure you want to raid Nahrain?*

Yes! he thought

Are you sure this mission is entirely political?

Yes!

There isn't anything of wounded pride?

No!

Then be it on your head. I warned you.

There was hesitation in him at that moment. She almost pitied him. Barad feared nothing. Except Seditha. What would it be like to live in fear of the goddess? And why did he fear her so? Hadn't she been munificent with him?

His hesitation lasted momentarily. Indecision hadn't won him a kingdom. And it wouldn't resolve this problem before him. An alliance between Oduman's two noble houses would be forged, whether that bitch Andulyn in Nahrain wanted to wed him or not.

There would be peace.

He signalled his generals. No quarter was to be given.

They rode down off the hill, onto the hard salt.

All of this for peace, for pride.

Oh, Barad, I did warn you.

Seditha's attention shifted to the city of Nahrain, to the palace, to a suite of rooms where lay the noblewoman Anduyn, asleep under down coverlets.

All these past days Andulyn, also, had visited the temple of Seditha, brought sacrifices, offered herself before the priestesses. Prayers of deliverance had been made. Prayers of supplication. Prayers of tears.

Andulyn's father sickened in his bed, vomiting, crying out against the pain of his limbs, and now had come those swellings under his arms and around his groin.

What Barad didn't know was that Nahrain was already a city in siege. And that Andulyn's prayers had been for her father first, and for the city second. It was this simple reason no response to overtures of marriage had been made. Barad's entourage had not been allowed to return.

But Seditha had warned Barad. All he could see was the smile of the goddess.

And so he rode. Peace out of war. This is what he told himself.

They came upon the white walls of Nahrain in a planned formation. Twenty of his best had gone on before, scaled the walls. It had been so simple. Few guards. Little fuss. The gates now swung open.

Another group slipped through, wound their way to the main stables, another to the markets, others to raid villagers' homes and disrupt movement in the streets. Barad led four teams toward the palace – to take out the guards, to hold the palace gates, to secure the way into Andulyn's rooms.

The others, the lesser captains and regular footmen, scythed through the narrow streets. The stables were secured. Horses ran shrieking from stalls now flame. Another team took and held the market square. Should dawn arrive and Barad still not have his quarry, they would be sure to prevent any amassing of people.

But it was here, in the square, the captain held his men, gorge in his throat. Where only hours from now should have been a babel of colour and wares, now stood a laden wagon, even in the moonless night grim in its cargo. Rats scurried over the shapes. It was then the captain realized there were rats aplenty in the square – dead, alive – hundreds of them there with the corpses. Beyond this, in a walled enclosure, was the glow of fire, the stink of burning flesh.

"Plague," one of the men whispered.

When his men bolted, the captain did nothing to stop them. Fighting was one thing. To die of plague was another.

He turned on heel, kicked a rat out of the way and fled.

In yet other districts of Nahrain soldiers ran in the grip of bloodlust, murdering, stealing, raping when there was occasion. Seditha watched it all dissolve into terror when Barad's men realized there was little resistance because people here had been dying before the raid.

Within the palace itself Barad met minimal opposition. His success sat heavily with him.

Worried, Barad? she asked.

He flinched, eyes darting. Light from wall braziers lit his face, his elaborate armour glinting. She might have thought to take him as a lover had he not been so in awe of her. She could have blessed him with gods for children.

But she let none of this touch him, only her concern.

This is too easy, he thought.

She smiled and he felt the bitterness of it, her warnings replaying in his mind.

Do you need to marry Andulyn that badly? she asked him now.

Yes!

Will a marriage without love be the foundation for peace?

Love has nothing to do with this.

Doesn't it? Perhaps you've been too long on the battlefield.

What's that supposed to mean?

That you long for conquest. I would have thought your harem sufficient.

It's not rutting I've in mind.

Again his glance darted. No guards. No opposition. This was too easy.

What trickery is this? he asked.

No trickery, Barad.

Then where are the guards?

Sick, dead, tending to their loved ones.

She felt a shudder run through him.

One of his men brought word Andulyn's rooms were secured.

He closed his eyes. *Seditha, please.*

I've giving you what you asked.

Yes. And I should be careful of what I ask.

You're learning, Barad.

He turned then and strode into Andulyn's rooms. Braziers burned brightly, the air hazy with incense, although underneath that heavy aroma lay another smell – sour, sickly. His gaze flashed to the windows where tapestries had been pulled. Everywhere there were remnants of medicaments, simples. He passed by scribes, councillors, leeches – all of them weary and beyond fear of him.

She watched him go into the main chamber where he found Andulyn on her knees, weeping over the body of her father, Dorain. Death was familiar to Barad. This Seditha knew. He recognized it quickly in Dorain. But what he wasn't prepared for was the manner of Dorain's death.

She felt his panic stir, heard his conclusions.

Plague. It was there in the swellings under Dorain's arms, in the smell of vomit under the incense.

Heat shot through him. She could feel him balance between fight or flight. But how to fight plague? And how to flee from it?

You warned me, Seditha.

She longed to embrace him, to return his arrogance and strength to him, but did nothing. It would have served nothing. If Barad were to forge peace in his kingdom he would have need of this.

But it would have soothed her to have given him peace.

I did warn you, Barad.

And I chose not to listen.

His resolve sharpened, focused. Fight. This was another enemy to him, she knew.

He inhaled sharply, bent, set his hands under Andulyn's shoulders and pulled her up, up, looked at her red-rimmed eyes so glazed, her mouth pale and trembling, aware of the swellings under her arms. And suddenly there was pain at the thought of this gentle maid dying.

Seditha wanted to cry out for his pain. So long she'd waited for some one person to touch him in the way no campaign could touch him. She only hoped Andulyn would.

"I could not answer you, my lord Barad," Andulyn said.

"I can see that." He touched her cheek to take the edge off his statement.

"I would have honoured you, my lord."

He could see the tears brim again in her eyes. Infected or not, he lifted her into his arms and carried her to her bed, ordering his men to make preparations for an honourable burial for Dorain, to bring him the leeches.

While he watched the leeches prepare an infusion of yellow powder and water, he questioned the councillors about what action was being taken in the city. This was fascinating to Seditha. Even now, when the man within him screamed out for Andulyn to heal, he knew his responsibility. The city needed him. Personal matters could wait. But for the first time Seditha could see him battle with himself.

Barad's reaction when the councillors informed him they were following Lady Andulyn's orders, gave Seditha further hope that at last Barad was ready for peace.

He knelt beside Andulyn then and asked her why she was having refuse collected from the streets, why it was necessary to burn the corpses, why she was opening baths for the people?

She touched his cheek, trembling, smiling at the way he worried. "I asked the goddess Seditha to show me how to save the people of Nahrain."

And she asked nothing for herself, Seditha said to him.

And because of this you'll let her die?

Accusation there. Now he feared this woman would die and leave him ignorant of her strength.

Afraid you'll lose your political alliance?

He studied Andulyn's face, amazed this small woman could bear herself so nobly in the face of so much death. Her first statement to him had been a veiled apology, her second a reassurance she would have honoured him.

No, Seditha - afraid I'll lose a cherished companion. And a teacher. There is so much I could learn from her, and share with her.

This sounds like love, Barad.

He touched Andulyn's fevered cheek, smiled. "I'll have your orders carried out, my lady."

Seditha smiled and this time Barad felt the warmth of the goddess, not the bitterness.

She won't die, Barad.

Am I such a stubborn man that you had to give me such hard lessons?

You already know the answer to that.

He laughed, drawing glances from his men. And laughed again. *Seditha, thank you. I am unworthy of the attention you give me.*

Don't insult me, Barad.

But she was laughing also when he bent and kissed Andulyn's lips - a liberty, a small token of affection, a sign of his faith in the goddess.

"You cannot return to the capital, my lord, "Andulyn said.

"I have no intention of returning to the capital until you are well and Nahrain is whole. Seditha has smiled upon us. With that I am content."

Seditha watched as he rose from Andulyn's side, unbuckled his armour and asked of the councillors where he could begin to work.

Figure 18: Digital painting, Lorina Stephens

And the Angels Sang

A Dishwasher for Michelina

For May it was unusually warm, which suited Sam Maloney just fine. The tomatoes were in the garden in record time. Already the carrots and parsnips sprouted, and the beans he'd planted two days ago cracked the earth.

What more could a man ask? – soil beneath his fingers, Michelina singing an aria from *Carmen* in the kitchen, his neighbour Caesere DiPaulo laughing next door. True, he could maybe ask for a little more money set aside, a better house out of Toronto, a dishwasher for Michelina. But he had his own home. Which was more than his da had. And his wife adored him. Which was more than Caesere had. And his boy Michael was a good boy. Which was more than most parents of sixteen year old boys had.

He straightened, wiping his hands on his jeans. Mike came through the back gate, calling a hello and commenting on the good mood of his mother. Sam laughed, thinking of the second dessert he and Michelina had shared.

Mike left him to have a shower. Sam listened to the night sounds around him – a siren, a car horn, a shriek. He thought again of what his son said earlier in the day, of money being able to buy you a dream, a little comfort. What dream could he buy on his wage from the abattoir? A brownstone house on a postage stamp lot?

Once more he berated himself for that degree he didn't have and realized the fact he was willing to numb his mind for eight hours a day bought no dreams. All his life was here in this garden, in the things he grew to fill their larder every year and fight the rising cost of living.

He left the humid night for his home, locked the doors and tucked himself around the curve of his wife's back.

☙❧

A Dishwasher for Michelina

Sam pedalled up the back lane the following evening, the stink of slaughter still in his head. They'd been processing pigs today. Even after twenty-four years the pigs bothered him.

He stashed the bike in the shed, locked up, swung open the gate and waved to Michelina who was visible in the kitchen window. As always, he paused for an inspection of his garden.

He bent closer to a rather luxuriant weed – two oval waxy leaves on a slender stem. It almost looked like a tree seedling. There was even a single coppery flower on it. He straightened, puzzling as he crossed the garden to the concrete patio, up the step and through the wooden screen door.

"Mia anima," Michelina said. "Good day? Tea or beer?"

He kissed her – three pecks, a small tradition. "Beer, please. It was a day."

Her dark eyes narrowed. "Pigs?"

He nodded.

She smiled compassionately. "Go shower. I'll bring you up a beer in a moment."

He set his lunch bucket on the counter. "What's for supper?"

"Salad and rolls." He glanced at the pork chops she'd been breading. She waved off his silent query. "It's too hot for pork chops anyway."

He smiled and kissed her again, patting her ample bottom.

"You two at it again?" Mike asked, leaning against the kitchen doorframe.

Sam straightened. Michelina laughed.

"Homework, son?" Sam asked.

"Just finished."

"Care to give me a hand identifying a plant after supper?"

"Sure. I'll have time before work. Whatcha got?"

"Don't know. Some odd weed in my tomatoes."

"I'll have a look while you're showering."

Sam turned and walked into the dim hall of papered beige flowers and old oak wainscoting, set his hand onto the smooth patina of the stair rail and climbed to the relief of a shower.

Dressed again, the taste of toothpaste in his mouth, he joined Mike in the living room at the wall of books.

"Strange plant, Pa," Mike said when Sam came beside him.

"My thoughts. Find anything?"

"Not so far."

"Been through the Audubon?"

"Yep. And the *Encyclopaedia of Trees, Petersen's*–"

"Nothing?"

"Nope." Mike snapped the book shut. "I think you've got a good one this time."

And the Angels Sang

Michelina called dinner. Over salad and rolls they discussed Sam's find. Michelina commented on the coppery flowers, plural, not singular, how pretty they were in the sunlight, like new pennies. Sam looked at her sharply. He kept his counsel and dipped his roll in the vinaigrette dressing in the bottom of his bowl.

After supper Mike grabbed another roll and left for work with his mother's admonishment on his heels. Sam mumbled something about him being a growing boy.

"He's going to grow us into a bigger grocery bill," Michelina said.

He left her clattering dishes. Once out in the garden he heard her singing *Quando m'en vo' soletta* from *La Bohème*. Caesere from next door leaned over the fence, which was a feat in itself. The fence was easily six feet high. Caesere was all of five-four.

"Buona sera," Caesere called.

"Evening," Sam answered, raising his gaze from the tomato patch.

"Some day at work today, eh?"

Sam nodded.

"Those pigs they squeal." He did a grating imitation.

"Shutup, Caesere."

"Can I borrow your seeder this weekend?"

"No problem. Let me know when you're ready." And when he was going to return it, along with his cordless hedge trimmer.

Caesere descended from his perch. Not long after Sam could hear Caesere's wife shouting imprecations about her husband's ability to do anything that didn't require a horizontal position. It made for interesting entertainment while he studied this oddity in his tomatoes.

Sam couldn't be sure, but he could swear the plant was at least two inches taller. There was definitely a change in the colour of one of the flowers, one silvery flower among three coppery. His nerves really skittered when he found a fresh new penny near the plant.

That did it. He shouted to Michelina he was going to the library, unlocked the shed and cycled off.

After three hours of research he achieved no more than to accumulate a mound of books around him that had the librarian twitching with anger. Apprehensive, he left the musty, golden interior of the library and stepped out into the humid night. He cycled slowly along Keele Street and opted for back routes home where the street lamps were older and the light more buttery than electric. He kept thinking how nice it would be to buy Michelina that dishwasher for her birthday in three weeks.

Back at the garden Mike waited for him, cross-legged on the grass, staring at the errant weed. "Something strange about that plant, Pa."

A Dishwasher for Michelina

Sam's heart fluttered as he joined his son.

"Sounds crazy, I know, but I could swear it's grown."

"Plants don't grow that fast." Even in the darkness Sam could see the seedling had grown, another two inches at least.

Michelina joined them now. She smiled and unfurled her palm. Five new pennies lay there, glistening. "I think your pocket needs mending," she said.

Sam fingered the in-tact lining where his hands had sunk. Were those flowers mostly silvery now? He turned and headed for bed, unable to watch that plant any longer.

Sleep proved hopeless. He ended up sitting out in the garden, watching the plant grow. Several times he heard the soft plunk of coins.

By noon the next day his head threatened explosion. All he could hear was the plunk of coins. He almost welcomed the slaughter of pigs. Anything to escape the impossibility he faced. When the buzzer blasted quitting time he lingered. He unhooked the hose, opened the valve and washed down the room again. What finally drove him home was the sight of water swirling down the drain.

So what if a money tree were in his garden? Didn't the Irish always look luck in the face?

Michelina waited by the gate to the alley. "Anima mia," she said. "I'm so glad you're home."

He swung off the bike, watching her face. Alarm there. Eagerness. This was so unlike Michelina. "What's happened?"

She shot a glance to either side. "Quickly."

He stored the bike, trying to control the tremor in his hands, the excitement he felt, knowing what he hoped was an impossibility.

There in the tomato patch, where there'd been a six inch seedling, was a three foot weed. It all but glowed with flowers. Some of those were now golden.

Just as last night, he heard a soft plunk. He looked down to a ring of pennies, nickels, dimes, quarters. And one very bright, very new, loonie.

Unable to believe what he saw, he pushed the leaves aside, searching for fruit and found in the thick foliage fruit in various stages of development, except this fruit could fill his larder in ways yet to be contemplated.

Another plunk sounded on the ground.

Caesere chose that moment for an over-the-fence chat. Both Sam and Michelina flinched, moved to block Caesere's line of sight.

"You're crazy," Caesere said. "Planting another tree."

Michelina giggled. He couldn't remember Michelina giggling, not like that. He reached for her hand.

"You should cut the other one down," Caesere said, shooting a greedy look at the maple.

"I like trees."

"Well maybe you can come rake all those leaves in my garden."

"And take away your wife's favorite topic of conversation?"

Caesere waved at him dismissively. "So what kind of tree you planted?"

A money tree. I didn't plant it, Caesere, it just grew. "Oh, it's a rare Australian fruit tree called lunaria munificentious." He almost cried out Michelina squeezed his hand so hard.

Caesere mumbled something incomprehensible in Italian and left his perch.

"We don't need him nosing around," Michelina hissed.

"He won't."

"But he is nosey."

"We'll just have to harvest constantly."

"Is this taxable income?"

He hadn't thought about that. It wasn't as if this was money from the bank, or the mint, or in some way he'd traded labour for wages. That didn't exactly make it income. It was more found money than income. And besides, what the Canada Revenue Agency didn't know wouldn't hurt him.

He bent and filled his pockets carefully, Michelina standing guard in case Caesere should decide to have another fence-side conference.

Over dinner the family discussed the fortuitousness of this find. Finally, Mike asked the question Sam had been avoiding: "How do we know the money isn't counterfeit?"

Michelina blushed. "It isn't."

Sam looked over at her.

She raised her hands as if to say she couldn't help herself and told them she'd spent loonies on milk this afternoon.

Sam sat there for a moment, and then: "I still can't help wonder where this plant came from."

"Maybe the University of Guelph might have an answer," Mike offered.

That was an excellent idea. Sam decided to call in sick the following day. He had two weeks leave he hadn't used. The next morning his call to Professor Edmund Everett at the UofG garnered nothing but derision. All Sam's other calls to the University of Toronto, the Royal Hamilton Botanical Gardens, the Toronto Horticultural Society were met with similar responses.

Disheartened, Sam took advantage of Michelina's trip to the grocer's and ordered a dishwasher from the Sears catalogue.

153

A Dishwasher for Michelina

A few minutes later he walked out to the garden. The money tree now measured six feet and fruited paper money in five and ten dollar denominations. Harvesting those was going to prove difficult. One stiff breeze and his fruit could end up all over the neighbourhood.

He plucked a ripe ten from a branch, fingering the purple bill so that it hissed like any ordinary new note. It was added to a roll he pulled from his pocket.

Maybe if he constructed a net to envelope the tree?

He spent the rest of the afternoon drawing up a plan for that, so when Michelina arrived home, three hours later than she should, he was only belatedly worried. Then disturbed.

Instead of groceries, she flounced in with an array of parcels, some from clothing stores from Yorkville and Hazelton Lanes. She made a great fuss about tipping the cabbie - a cabbie! - and told him to leave the bundle buggy on the curb for the garbage.

She'd obviously been to a salon. Her hair was cut. He looked at his hands and already missed the feel of it. Her face was made up in one of those re-do jobs - black eyeliner, red lipstick. Somehow the fact she was overweight never bothered him before. But now she looked like she belonged on Queen Street.

Michelina didn't wear lipstick for chrissakes!

She smiled and pulled a black lace corset from one of the brightly coloured bags.

"What are you going to do with that?" he managed to ask.

She licked her lips. "Wear it, mia anima."

Oh. He glanced at the other bags, wondering if she'd also bought a leather play suit. All he wanted was Michelina in a plain rose housecoat, slippers on her feet, sleep in her face. He didn't want this, this ....

"You don't like it," she said.

"Well now, darlin', it's em, sort of - "

"You don't like it."

"I like it fine, darlin'. It just doesn't seem quite, well, you."

"Well it is now." She laughed and dumped the froth of lace back into the bag, gathered parcels into her arms and almost skipped up the stairs.

"What about groceries?" he yelled after her.

"I've ordered Chinese."

Chinese. Ordered it. He couldn't remember the last time they'd ordered in food. And as if Chinese tonight was going to give him breakfast in the morning, or lunch at work. Shit. He didn't even like Chinese.

He turned and walked back out to the money tree. The fact it budded olive green flowers along with red and brown did nothing to ease his mood.

And the Angels Sang

He poked a little further and found one solitary, very lovely mauve flower. A thousand dollar note about to fruit.

He glanced up at their bedroom window, Michelina's rich voice sweeping out into the sunlight. Puccini this time. The dishwasher seemed like an insignificant gift now. She only sang Puccini when she was in a very good mood.

She leaned out the window. "Forgot to tell you. Ordered new appliances while I was out. Jen-airs."

Jen-airs. He'd settled for Sears Kenmore.

He slumped cross-legged on the ground, listening to her sing, to Caesere's wife yell, to the birds in the maple. A siren sounded somewhere, probably over from Dundas way. It occurred to him there would be some adjustments to riches. Wealth he could comprehend, but riches obviously would require a shift in gears.

Why did Michelina find it so easy?

Sam looked up from his contemplation of the ground to find Mike grinning from ear to ear. "Good day at school?"

"Great."

Why did he feel another bomb about to drop? "Oh?"

"Yeah. Just called that old geeser Franklin at the donut shop."

"Oh?"

"I quit."

"What do you mean you quit?"

"I don't need a job now."

"And why is that?"

"We're gonna be rich."

"So that gives you the right to just walk out on an obligation?"

"Geez, Pa. It's not like I owe Franklin anything."

"You owe him some respect."

Mike rolled his eyes and stalked off to the house. Sam knew he should call the boy back, dress him down, reason this out.

What the hell was happening here?

The first twenty unfurled and fluttered down to Sam's feet.

                         ❧❦

There was tai dop voy, honey garlic chicken wings, shrimp chop suey, soo guy, at least another dozen dishes on the table, and this with egg rolls, fortune cookies and those little plastic packages of soya sauce. As if everything didn't already have enough sauce. Including Michelina. This was her fourth glass of wine. Not that rot-gut her father always sent over. Real wine, with a cork, from the liquor store.

A Dishwasher for Michelina

Probably this dinner cost a hundred bucks easy. Why should he worry? It wasn't as if his money didn't grow on trees. He peered into the globe of garnet wine in his hand, wondering why he didn't feel elated by all this.

"So when do the new appliances arrive, Ma?"

Sam stared at his son over the top of his wine glass.

Michelina giggled. "Tomorrow afternoon." She turned to Sam. "You'll have to get those old things out of here by then, mia anima."

"I will?"

"Yes. I'm sure the delivery men won't."

"And what am I supposed to do with them?"

She giggled again, giving her son a conspiratorial look. "Well I don't know. That's your job."

"Oh? And what's yours?"

"Keeping things in order."

As if he weren't capable of organizing himself. "They'll have to drop the new ones in the hall. I'll move the old ones when I get home tomorrow."

"Home?"

"Yes. I do have a job, you know. It's what's paid the mortgage all these years."

"Well I don't see why you have to keep that job now."

"Yeah, Pa. Ma's right. With that tree – "

"I'm keeping my job."

They both stared at him. Michelina smiled after a moment, one of her now-let's-not-get-overexcited smiles. "Well, maybe I can get one of the construction crew to move the old appliances tomorrow."

"Construction crew?"

"I'm sure I told you. We're having the house renovated: a larger kitchen, a sun room – "

"And where is all this renovating going?"

"It's going in the garden."

"But I like the garden."

"Well, yes, you can still have a small patch, enough for the money tree – "

"You didn't even ask me."

"Well I didn't think you'd mind."

"And just how much fruit do you think that tree's going to bear?"

"Lots, Pa. Just look how much we've gotten in just these few days."

He threw his napkin onto the plate. "I don't believe I'm hearing this. Nothing," he pointed to Michelina, "do you hear me? Nothing is to take place until I get home tomorrow. Not one brick. Not one wall. Nothing is to be changed." He stomped from the room into the hall. He was going to escape to the garden. But that damned tree was in the garden. Instead, he climbed the stairs and lay on the bed in the darkness, listening to whispers below him, to whispers in Caesere's yard, to whispers in his head.

A money tree. A money tree. A money tree.

He barely stirred at all when Michelina crawled into bed. What did wake him was the sound of Caesere laughing.

Sam sat straight up in bed.

There it was again. Soft. Sneaky. It almost sounded as if the laughter came from his own garden.

Carefully, he swung his legs over the bed and padded to the window. Sure enough, there in the garden he could make out the shape of a man. That did it. He didn't mind lending. But he sure as hell wouldn't tolerate stealing.

He made his way down the hall, opened Mike's bedroom door, managed to find the bat without tripping over the obstacle course, and was out in the garden.

Caesere gasped when Sam touched his shoulder.

"Hey, Sam. Comme esta?"

Sam glanced down at the bulging plastic bag in Caesere's hand. "You could have asked."

Caesere's face hardened. "Yeah, well, in Corsica we take what we need."

"This isn't Corsica."

The little man postured. "So whadya going to do? Hit me?"

Sam nodded to the fence. "Get out of here."

With that Caesere turned and scampered over the fence, laughing under his breath.

Sam sank to the dew-damp grass, the bat across his knees, and kept guard.

❧❦

He'd left Mike in charge of guarding the tree when he hiked off for work, feeling somewhat relieved, only to find when he got to work his boss left a message attached to his time card.

In all the years he'd worked at the abattoir, he couldn't ever remember meeting the president of the company. Not personally. He'd had glimpses when the big boy brought people through for a tour. But he'd never exchanged so much as a word.

Nervously, he stood in the wood-panelled office of Mr. Podmorski's secretary.

"Mr. Podmorski will see you now," the woman said.

She opened the door onto a mahogany panelled office, brass wall sconces gleaming, a window that looked out over the rail yards. Podmorski, large with a shining pate, sat behind a mahogany desk in a brown leather chair that squeaked when he rose to shake Sam's hand. The grin on his face left Sam wary.

"I'll get right to the point, Sam." Sam. Not Maloney. "You've been a valuable employee and now we'd like an opportunity to show you our appreciation."

"How is that?"

"We'd like to give you an opportunity to buy in." He lifted a glossy report. "Our fiscal statements are very good. And a wise man like you, well, I'm sure–"

"Who told you?"

The report seemed to wilt in Podmorski's hand. "I beg your pardon?"

"Who told you?"

"I'm sure I don't know what you're talking about."

"Caesere DiPaulo told you."

"DiPaulo? Does he work here?"

"I may not have a degree, but I'm not stupid. Caesere DiPaulo asked you for an interview yesterday. I know. The whole plant was talking about it."

"Well, yes, I seem to recall having a meeting – "

"And he told you I'd recently come into a sizable ... inheritance."

"That may have come about in small talk."

"It was the talk. I'm not interested. You didn't even know my name until yesterday." He nodded to the fiscal report. "And as for that, I do read. I've seen what the *Globe & Mail* wrote about a certain failing meat processing plant. You can't buy me. I quit."

He rose with Podmorski sputtering, turned and stalked down to the locker rooms. Questions rose behind him like a wave. Caesere cornered him, grinning, plainly pleased with himself. Sam said nothing. He left with his lunch bucket in hand.

By the time he cycled into his shed he knew things at home weren't going to be much better. Where had been a burgeoning spring garden was now a field of reporters, all of them racing toward him, microphones aimed like stun guns. Questions shot off like rocket fire.

Somehow he managed not to deck any of them and shouldered his way to the back door. Inside there was no relief either. Michelina giggled. Sam groaned.

"There's a reporter from CITY TV to interview you," she said.

"No interviews."

"But, Sam. This is important – "

He glared at her. With a count of ten under his tongue, he entered his living room, found a camera crew set up, sound technicians hovering. A

And the Angels Sang

man in a grey suit sat in his chair. His chair. Rose up to greet him. Lights burst into whiteness. He squinted, shielding his eyes.

"My. Maloney, pleased to meet you, I'm - "

"No interview. Out."

"But, Mr. Maloney, Mrs. Maloney said - "

"Said shit. No interview. Out."

"If you'd just answer - "

"Out."

"How much have you harvested - "

"God Damn You! Get out!"

The reporter smirked and nodded to the crew. Within moments they were out into the morass of journalists demolishing his front lawn. Briefly he heard something about the evening news.

Enough. He fanned through the yellow pages for a security firm, found one and was on the phone. There'd be a team there in the morning.

Sam went to bed before the evening news.

The following morning he thought maybe things were going to be all right. An armed guard now stood watch under the money tree that had reached a height of twenty feet, and another stood sentinel outside the front door until the video cameras could be linked into the house system. A team from the same firm set up the latest high-tech around the property. They were even having his phone number changed to a private listing.

He smiled and sat back on the kitchen chair, tugged the robe over his knees and sipped coffee.

What he didn't expect was a phone call from the mayor. Seems there was a historical restoration project on which the city was working, and Sam could assist with a generous donation. Sam left the mayor talking when he quietly hung up the receiver.

The guard from the front door signalled him over the portable house phone. "There's a team here from the University of Guelph, Mr. Maloney."

"Send them away."

In the background he could hear his son on the other phone placing an order with an electronics store.

Sam took his coffee and sat out on the back porch, looking at the desolation of his garden. The only things left standing were the old maple and the money tree. Everything else - the extensive perennial beds, the roses, the vegetables, even the little bird bath and fountain he had in the middle of the strawberries - were in ruins. He watched a thousand dollar bill drift down into the net around the money tree.

Later in the day he made a phone call to a business machine dealer where he ordered a computer for immediate delivery, and made another phone call

A Dishwasher for Michelina

to Manitoulin Island. It was amazing how quickly business could be concluded when money was not an issue.

❧

The clock in the hall just struck two a.m. when Sam slipped out of bed and padded his way into the kitchen where he'd stowed a pair of jeans and his sneakers. He dressed and punched in the clearance code at the back door alarm.

Humidity clung to his arms like a wet blanket when he stepped outside. The gardener's basket in his hands seemed too conspicuous. He glanced over to Caesere's. No lights.

The guard at the money tree turned to him.

"It's just me," Sam said. "Go take a break. I'll watch for awhile."

"Can't sleep, Mr. Maloney?"

"Too humid."

"If you're sure it's okay?"

Sam waved him off. "Fine. Fine. Way you go. Think I'll just do some fixing up out here."

The guard nodded gratefully and slipped through into the kitchen.

Sam worked quickly with those few minutes he had. When the guard came back he handed over a crinkling hundred dollar bill. "Boredom pay."

The guard grinned. "Thanks, Mr. Maloney."

Sam smiled and went back into the house. In the kitchen he sorted his harvest, added that to the stash he'd hidden in the freezer in foil packages marked dough. The cuttings he wrapped carefully in damp peat and plastic, then foil and scrawled cutlets across the top, and stored them in the meat keeper. Removing the label from the bottle of herbicide proved trying, but in the end it came off and he washed all those bits down the drain. The jug he shredded with scissors and recycled it.

Later, when Michelina and Mike decided to get up, he'd tell them about Manitoulin. They couldn't argue. And even if they did the movers would be here by noon and his family could come or not. Until then he planned just where he'd plant the new seedlings he'd grow from those cuttings. Fifteen thousand hectares of forest would be room enough to hide a few trees. And if Michelina joined him, he might even get her that dishwasher.

Figure 19: Pen & ink sketch, Lorina Stephens, previously published, The Standing Stone, 1990

A Memory of Moonlight and Silver
Published previously, The Standing Stone, 1990

Her hands! Her hands! Be sure to tie her hands!"

"I am, Captain."

"Be quick about it."

"I can't go any faster than fast."

"It only takes these elves a twitch to kill."

The soldier yanked the rope around her wrists. "I've no more desire to see elven power than you."

She did everything to make it plain to the captain she wouldn't accept her recapture. To have shown him her fear would be dangerous.

The little man, the soldier, tossed her up to the front of the captain who was horsed. Their handling wasn't gentle. She chewed on the bruises she'd received over the endless days of running, determined to show them nothing.

It was plain the captain not only didn't trust her ability to cast a killing spell, but her innate ability with animals, in that her hands had been tied behind her back, further limiting their use. Moreover, it was an uncomfortable way to ride. Her shoulders ached. She longed to relieve the strain. His leather jerkin stank and she was grateful when they set into a trot, although every movement jarred her bones. The fall wind numbed her face, her limbs so cold she instinctively pressed her back to the captain's chest for warmth. She would steal what she could.

A sudden change in weather had lowered her caution last night. With the night so cool she hadn't thought Raxis' men would continue the chase. That had been her only mistake. For eight days she'd evaded them, now only to be taken back to that mountain peasant who called himself king.

The captain laughed. She knew that kind of laughter.

"Raxis will be pleased."

The solider nodded. "For awhile at least."

"What's the matter? You've no stomach for elven misery?"

"They cry just like humans."

And the Angels Sang

"There's nothing human about an elf. Just look at her. Any human would be afraid of what's going to happen when she gets back. But this thing! She sits here in front of me like a block of wood."

What would he know of wood? When was the last time he'd felt a tree scream at the cut of an axe?

"Maybe she's in shock. It was awfully cold last night."

"Shock nothing. She's an elf I tell you. Don't let that silver face of hers bewitch you."

"I'm no fool, Captain."

"So be warned. Let down your guard with this one and she'll kill you before you can regret it."

The captain lied. That she knew. But the soldier had no understanding of his lies. There was no way she could tell him elves didn't' kill ... at least when it wasn't necessary. That wasn't their way. The soldier's silence came as a relief.

For most of the day they twisted along the mountain road, the arches of golden leaves hissing in the bitter wind. There were few travellers, mostly merchants and minstrels. Those who trudged down the mountain were plainly discouraged by the king's response. She wondered at that. Had he become so obsessed with her recapture that he ignored his people's demands? Was the castle closed to trade? If that were so, things wouldn't go well for her there. She could only hope for an opportunity to escape in the next three nights. It would take that long for the full moon, and it was necessary for her to be in Fionelthen, her home, by then.

They made camp that night in a circle of beech trees. She sat cross-legged, staring into the fire, her tattered cloak fluttering like broken feathers. Firelight softened her silver hair. It did nothing to warm the coldness she felt inside. The men left her to her silence. They watched her suspiciously, judging her with prejudice, but she did nothing to make them comfortable. Her gaze remained hooded, unwavering, almost as if she were in charge at this camp. It wasn't overlong before they turned their attention to their comfort.

The captain and the soldier dined on iron rations and a skin of wine. It had been days since last she'd eaten anything of substance. The scant meals of berries and roots kept her alive, but they did nothing to fill the empty hole that was her stomach. Want pushed her to speak.

"You'll have to feed me if you want Raxis to see me alive."

The captain glared at her, his dark beard sparkling with wine. He elbowed the soldier.

"What, me feed her?"

"You will if you want to stay under Raxis' favour."

Grumbling, the soldier crept toward her. He was pitiful in his attempt to hide his trembling, but she knew to show him pity would be compromising. When he shoved a strand of dried flesh between her teeth she bit him.

He was still inventing new names for her when the captain said, laughing, "Re-tie her hands in front of her. If she wants to eat she can feed herself."

"But— "

"Be quick about it. Remember what I said before about her hands."

The soldier did as he was ordered, although his reluctance was evident in the way he worried the ropes. Despite herself she flinched, her wrists burning anew from his roughness. He left her little room for movement. She would find a way to take advantage of that meagre freedom. Necessity had made her economic in her needs.

Her meal was unsatisfying. Even a loaf of elven journey bread would have been better than what they offered. The memory of her former life again stirred. It was always like a shadow at her shoulder. She would not think of that life now. What she didn't need was one of her moods. That would only quench the flame that drove her, obsessed, almost reckless; it was something required of her.

As they ate she studied her captors. They mistrusted her because of her elvenness. In another time it could have been otherwise, another time before Raxis' dungeons. There she had been feared even by other prisoners. The stone rang with their jeers, their fears and at times with their violence. Elven sympathizers died from dungeon fever. There had been those sleepless nights, when the moon silvered her cell, she'd heard the infection work. She shuddered inwardly with memory.

Firelight glinted off the men. Their skin shone with grease, like stuffed pigs she thought as they talked in murmurs behind the russet flames. Woodsmoke scorched her eyes. Her body still twitched from the sapling they'd cut for firewood, smoky and green as it was. Idiots. It had been useless to warn them of the pain they'd cause to both the tree and to her, and in the end she knew either pain would have been of no concern to them. Elven lore they'd called her protests, nothing more than legends and witchery. They'd have no part of her evil. At one point they'd crossed themselves furtively and rechecked her bonds. The rope around her wrists seemed to assure them of safety, so much they hadn't even bothered to bind her ankles.

Perhaps they should feel safe. Why hobble her when to bolt was useless? She had been eight days without sufficient food and rest, eight days tortured by the threat of recapture. Her legs would give out before she tried to run. They could drag her back before she made it a bowshot away. What she needed was a little of that elven lore. The way the men talked, she was sure

Raxis meant to annihilate every last elf, and life to her was still precious. Perhaps she should consider a plea.

But she was elven, prideful; honour would prevent her.

She ate their food, stole warmth from their fire, and waited.

When night sealed the wood, the men nodded by the fire. Wind spun through the canopy, hushing the sounds of darkness and scoured a chain of sparks from the blaze. She remained cross-legged, testing the strength of the moon as it rose. In another three nights it would be full. She couldn't wait another three nights; if ever she were to escape it was now, even though she could not be hopeful. She would try. Necessity drove her to try.

She pressed her fingertips into a triangle and counted away time till the moon crested the beeches. She threw glances at her nodding captors. At any moment something in the forest could stir, rouse the men, and her opportunity would be gone. Just a little higher, a little more, just ride the tops of the trees ....

There!

The triangle of her fingers shadowed her forehead. A beam of silver filled that shape. She lidded her eyes to concentrate, because she would need all her strength if she were to succeed tonight. Such a spell required free use of her hands, a piece of elven silver and lore greater than she had ever used. All she had was determination. The light inside the triangle cooled her head. She let that silver light absorb her, clothe her.

Slowly she chanted, "Eldoroth esputh sethspes," over and over again till the trees vibrated to the clear sound of her voice. The circle filled with argence, like a well feeding from a spring. The leaves themselves seemed to whisper those three elven words. Too late the men realized what she did. They slept without dreams by a fire that burned like silver leaves.

Her arms fell. She nursed the pain in her body. The spell had been greater than she – her worst fear – and she, also, slept by the enchanted fire, victim of her exhaustion.

She woke. Dawn defined the colours beneath her a warm-hued carpet of leaves through which moss rose like green tufts of fur. It made her think of Fionelthen. How long had it been since she'd been home? Watched the colours change with the day, mitigating their claim on the land? There was nothing more pleasing than to see the elf-stones blush at dawn, the leaves of the trees all golds and greens, each like a sun. At midday their world was brilliant, blue and emerald, the musty smells of earth and bark reminding them of their origins. Perhaps the most pleasant was during the full moon when everything seemed forged of ancient silver. It was the most magical of all. The elves always were partial to silver.

That's why the elven lord called her Eltheniel. It meant elven silver. A powerful name. She remembered power. Its remnants were still in her fingers, her long, silver-white fingers that once spun moon-threads into elven cloth.

She glanced at the cloth of her clothes, wrinkling her nose. What ever happened to the elven cloth she wore? Did some saucer-eyed maiden wear it to Raxis' bed?

She whirled, her mouth dry with dread.

She scrambled to her feet. Her gaze shot to the snoring men. Anxious and tired, she crept through the leaves to the horses, hoping the spell of the fire would last long enough to give her some distance. With a gentle word she mounted and was off. Just how far Fionelthen was she was unsure, but she would journey until she found it.

She travelled, reluctant to meet any humans, in a wood which hemmed a common thoroughfare. Her course took her through the trembling hills of aspen until mid-morning, although she paused twice to cast a spell of silence around herself. There had been riders on the road, their horses heavy and bay, glinting with brasses and armours as gaudy as jays. These men – at least she was sure they were men – wore armour which would have been their deaths had they fallen. So much encumbrance for a fighter. How could they fight so encumbered? But there, twice where the road dipped deeply into the woods, they reined in, their harsh tongues clattering. Even their horses seemed annoyed as they pawed the ground. Appreciation of grace wasn't something unique to elves. Horses knew of this also. It had been so plain to her the animals only wished to pasture. Had she been their steward ....

But she was not.

For some time the two soldiers batted words between themselves. She was sure they glimpsed her. Had it not been for her spell and her elven knack of stillness she and her mount would have been found. Of that she was sure. Could it be Raxis searched this hard for her?

But of course he would. She had knowledge he coveted enough to spend lives extravagantly – human or elven, it made little difference.

Three hundred survivors had made that arduous journey to his high mountain kingdom when Raxis routed them from Fionelthen. They had marched, tethered like a flock of pheasants. He had been sure to bind their hands, some small insurance against spells.

But Raxis hadn't been quick enough immobilizing her. It was for that reason she fretted to return to Fionelthen, lost as she was. Her task, and her journey, would end there.

Eltheniel searched her memory after the riders retreated, trying to find some clue as to her path and directions.

For awhile she watched the place the knights had been, thinking. She abandoned her thoughts. Testing her way, she nudged her mount to the road. Kicked among the leaves was an object that gleamed of silver. It was all she could do to keep her hands steady and she swung her leg over the horse and down to the ground, to bend, to grasp the lovely thing between her fingers. She blinked. This was too fortunate. She blinked again. She straightened, her hair caught in an errant breeze.

Silver lay in the palm of her hand like a wish. This was no ordinary harness flash. This was something from her people, a harness flash of silver emblazoned with a crescent moon and a broad oak. This was nothing less than a trapping from her father's treasury. Elven silver was not ordinary silver.

She indulged in a smile, yanking loose the leather string from her jerkin and looping the flash securely. With her find at her breast, she hauled back up the horse and slipped back into the wood. She made better distance that day than she had in any other, and this time she found a few places familiar; whether because she had wandered this way during her escape, or whether she was on the path to Fionelthen, she was unsure.

Night was well-woven through the trees when she climbed an oak and made an elven nest for herself, her horse set loose with a command not to stray too far. With sweet cicely, rosehips and walnuts filling her belly, she slept before moonrise. All things considered it was a better camp and a better meal than that of the previous evening.

Moonlight stirred her. The moon rose large and silver, flattened at one edge where it had yet to bloom. She hummed, her back against the bark, her fingers steepling into a triangle around the silver flash she'd found.

The object trembled with moonlight, growing in brilliance until her hands were brilliant. She dared not hope. Like spider's legs her forefingers knitted the silver light, at first testing the air and then slowly, as the moon rose, a strand grew from the loop of the flash.

Knitting moonlight into silver was something that stirred a long-ago life. The wonder of it filled her as it had that first time in a distant autumn. There had been laughter as light as the silver they spun. Even the elven lord and lady laughed that night. They had all laughed – the spinning children, the elders, the parents, the lord and lady.

Eltheniel stared at the thread in her hand. There was no laughter tonight. How could she laugh without someone to share her success? There was only the throb in her head for company. She cried herself to sleep in the cradle of the tree, the silver cold against her breast.

She woke wet from a drizzle that had swept through the night. And froze. Two horses snuffled beneath her. Their scent rose sweetly, teasing her nose.

Caution stayed her from inhaling, deeply as she wanted; there was another smell with the horses. It, unlike the animal's, was not sweet. It was the foul stench of men. She peered through the leaves. Beneath her were two riders. It wasn't difficult to hear what they discussed.

"We can't be sure she came this way," the dark haired one said.

The other snorted. "You heard the talk among the villagers: *Moonlight pouring like a river into the wood.* There's only one thing I know of that will do that."

"An elf."

The other nodded.

She bit the curse on her tongue. How could she have been so careless?

"An elf with elven silver," said the dark one, "and you just happened to lose that flash yesterday."

So these were the same two soldiers. They obviously found their armour an encumbrance, dressed as they were now in breaches, shirts and iron-ringed leather jerkins. That meant urgency and need of some speed.

"So she has elven silver," said the other. Eltheniel marked the bitterness on his face. This one was a hunter. "We can still take her."

"Indeed? Have you ever stopped an elf with elven silver? Look what she did to those two dolts, and that was without silver. Don't be a lunatic."

"We wait for her at Fionelthen."

"What?"

"We wait for her at Fionelthen. Now that she has elven silver, it's an easy guess she'll head for home. Why not wait for her there instead of chasing behind her?"

The dark one grinned. Eltheniel thought of a wolf. The soldiers would make dangerous travelling companions, but with the right spell and a little luck she could have them lead her home. Why not use their knowledge when hers lacked?

They continued to chatter for some time before they reined their horses around and headed westward through the wood. She waited until they were stumps in the distance and leapt from her nest. With a whicker from her lips she brought her mount back from its wandering and as best she was able cautioned it to silence.

Throughout the day she played a game of hide and seek. She needn't have been so cautious about silence. The soldiers created enough noise to alarm a village and that puzzled her after awhile. Surely they knew about keen elven senses. Were they so sure they'd find her at Fionelthen that they tossed caution aside? It was then she realized they might wait until nightfall to search for her. She had been recaptured at night. And she had been located because of her weakness for moonlight. That was a mistake she wouldn't repeat.

Her stealth excited her that day. What with the golden day around her, dripping with warmth, her confidence grew. She was, after all, an elf. Listen to her senses and she might be successful against these humans. It wasn't that she wanted a battle. Battles were something she faced with reluctance; she chose to fight out of necessity, not desire, and she couldn't help but wish that Raxis left the elves alone. They hadn't harmed him. In fact they'd retreated and retreated from human association until there had been only one last haven – Fionelthen. Not even magic had been enough against those human numbers, and the elves had been governed by conscience. She couldn't heed conscience now. There was neither time nor luxury for conscience.

Twilight came swiftly to the forest. She remained cloaked in shadows as the soldiers made their way down to a road where meadow was bathed in sunset. At some small distance gleamed the first lamps of evening in a village. As she despaired might occur, they were intent upon taking their evening at the village inn – a place she couldn't go, not with her silver-white face, grey eyes and pale hair. A dog ran barking at their heels, warning villagers of strangers. Soon the place would be astir. She turned, taking what welcome the forest afforded. Tomorrow she would take up their trail once more.

She delved into the trees for some distance, climbing several hills which folded one upon another in a gradual ascent. Here the aspen and beech waned, giving way to birches that wove through the darkness like faded bones. She paused to take a little of the papery bark.

Night was falling swiftly now but it caused her little difficulty as she relied upon her acute vision to guide her way. She didn't look back. That would have been to yield to despair, for she had come a long way.

After some steep climbing, over dead logs burdened with new growth and dense holly brush, she came upon a severe descent where she reluctantly set free her horse. Here the darkness was absolute. Not even her elven sight aided her and she peered cautiously through the emerald veil. She sniffed the air. Water was there, walnuts also, far down in the bowl of the valley.

It took no small effort to descend without falling. Dew was heavy upon the leaves. Her thin boots afforded her little traction and more than once she slid, her hands clawing for purchase. Finally she found herself on level ground, in a pool of moonlight where a pond shone like a silver coin, threaded in shadow from an ancient walnut tree.

The invitation to bathe was almost more than she could deny. Yet deny she did. Here were goods which would yield her some small measure of disguise and an opportunity to converse with her pursuers.

Assured by distance and the depth of the valley, she bent and gathered fallen wood, touching the trees with gratitude as she went. The fire she built was small, enough to give her warmth. Near to her she had gathered a collection of odds bits – leaves and nuts from the walnut, a few rocks, and a shred of birch bark. She leaned toward the fire, nesting a rock near the embers. Around that flat slab she placed the others, filling in with an assortment of pebbles. Next she stripped off her cloak at the water's edge and scooped dripping handfuls of mud from the pond and dumped them onto the cloth. With this she packed the small ring of stones she had made, her long fingers moving hastily. A few times she swore when heat seared her flesh. But she kept working.

When at length the stones were sealed with the black sludge, she settled cross-legged and waited for the mud to bake. Her eyes were weighted with sleep, the fire warm. Twice she caught herself nodding and awoke with a start. She rose, pacing around her camp, restless, her gaze darting to the shadows around her. Things scuttled, drawn by the fire. She let them be. They were no harm, only curious.

When the crude pot paled she carried mouthful after mouthful of water to the fire, spitting her cargo into the vessel. To that she added torn bits of walnut leaves, cracked and mashed nuts, and the shredded birch bark. She stirred the brew carefully, adding water as more boiled away, always refraining from using any kind of elven power. Although safe in the valley, she wanted no attention drawn to her. Better to use wood-lore than elven.

The moon was setting by the time she kicked out the fire and let the stones cool. Her fingers twined into her pale hair, combing it through as best she could and reluctantly, slowly, she dipped the ends into the dark liquid. It was cooling quickly now, quickly enough that she could stand the heat. More and more of her hair was doused in the foul-smelling dye, each time emerging brown. When at last there was only the top of her hair to tint, she almost sat on her head, splashing more of the dye onto her face to dull her pale complexion. There was nothing she could do about her eyes she knew. With luck the humans would mistake her for a wandering northern bard.

She sat beside the last few embers, her hair splayed around her in dark strands, drying. With a sharp stone she carved herself a flute out of a hardened hollow reed. Periodically she tested it, plugging one hole, carving a little further on. That she was hungry wasn't important. This disguise might purchase more than necessity.

By the time the birds tittered in the trees, she had completed her night's task, without sleep, and stood staring at her reflection in the pond. What she saw was unlike any image she'd had of herself. Even darkened, her hair seemed not her own, matted, filthy, woven with bits of ash, leaf and twig like some fey adornment. Her eyes were hard in the reflection, granite. Bones pressed her face into harsh lines. There was something smouldering in her face, a relentless drive that pushed her beyond all restraint. This was not the Eltheniel she had last seen.

That had been a mirror in her room, she dressed in woodland colours for a woodland trek, what was to have been a scouting mission unknown to her father. The elven lord never risked her, although she was capable. She had been his only heir, and to risk her was to put everything at risk. She had been looking in the mirror when Raxis' troops put Fionelthen to siege.

She turned her back on the stranger in the pond and set herself to the hills.

It would bring her no advantage to stop at the inn on her way through the village. She had no money to purchase breakfast, and certainly to play for her meal would have been fine for evening; questionable for morning. And she needed the advantage of wines and ales in weary men to win her case. Instead, she chose to slip into an outlying farm, stealing a few clothes from a line. The garments fit her near enough, although a little short in the arm and leg. She could expect nothing else from human tailors. They never sewed for elves.

The two soldiers had returned to the road and it wasn't difficult to find them, shadowing their path as she did in the trees. Here the land was familiar. It must be the same woods that reached to Fionelthen. There would be no risk of running out of trees, and that relaxed her caution. Only a little. She still travelled through human territory, a hunted criminal by virtue of her race.

Deciduous trees thinned here, giving way to an abundance of cedars that cast a thick gloom and provided scant cover. To her dismay the soldiers rode into the forest, cracking the lower dead branches as they went, still unconcerned for the noise they made. More and more it taxed her to stay silent. Her body trembled with hunger, exhaustion. When they broke bread while riding she almost cried out with want, but held herself. There would be time yet.

Toward late afternoon they made a gradual descent back to the road. The land was rank with the smell of decay, swamp, and other odours that betrayed human lodgings. She waited in the cedars as they rode toward a rickety collection of frame buildings, all in need of repair and skill. One, larger than the others, rose upon water-stained stilts. A doubtful staircase meandered up one grey side, opened to a landing where it seemed lodgings were kept, and then pushed upward again to a single, weathered door. A sign, faded and barely legible, hung akimbo over the muddy path. Elven Cross.

Her heart lurched. It seemed impossible she might be this close to home, and yet the land was all too familiar now. She knew that a little further along the road would be a T-junction. There would be the road to home. And a task she didn't want to complete.

The soldiers entered the inn. She stepped out of cover, her flute in hand, and struck out for the derelict building. There might be hope of gaining some information about Raxis.

The wind had turned colder, biting through her coarse, woollen garments. The cloak proved poor shelter. Her thin boots dampened quickly in the mud and she went with caution, afraid she might lose her footing and tumble. The dye couldn't survive that. Should she get wet she would be undone.

A little further along the road she could just make out the junction. Swamp had claimed most of the road where it plunged down into the water before climbing a large, mangy hill. The cedars ended abruptly there. She turned her gaze away. This side of the road was straw-coloured, tatty; even the thin cows that grazed were poorly-kept. The shed which had once sheltered them now was in ruin. She couldn't remember there ever being a farm, let alone an inn, here. In the few years she'd been away so much had happened. Perhaps they'd even torn Fionelthen down stone by stone. She pulled the cloak closer to her body.

It was plain the village wanted. All the buildings were as pathetic as the inn, the children who scrabbled in the mud hard, menacing. When she reached the stairs, the village's wiry smith tumbled down, cursing as he rolled and glared at her when he finally sprawled in the mud. She merely stepped over him, testing the questionable stairs. Children's taunts ringed the smith. Better they gave him their attention than her.

The door swung inward at the touch of her fingers, creaking. She inhaled sharply; the smells, although warm, were oppressive, as those of her prison had been. It had been both a longing to smell elven things and a need to complete a spell that had driven her to use magic and moonlight the night she escaped. Then, as the night she'd charmed her captors with sleep, it had almost cost her freedom.

A block of evening sun fell through the door, framing her. The cacophony halted. Quickly she closed the wood and the animation resumed; she breathed, aware of how frightened she had been. For a moment longer she stood there, scanning the beamed room and was finally drawn toward the blaze upon the hearth. That, at least, offered her some cheer. And some reward. Her pursuers were seated at a long table, bent toward one another.

Eltheniel swallowed her fear and strode toward the fire, setting a stool near the hearthstones for warmth. The soldiers paid her no more than a cursory glance. That suited her fine. She leaned into the fire, her hands fanned to gather warmth. A blackened pot hung there, bubbling something savoury. Her mouth watered.

The innkeeper was occupied with one of the villagers, and she took advantage of that to draw out her flute and blow the first reedy chords of something soothing. The soldiers passed her frequent looks now. She shifted into a lively tune and that ended their conversation. By now others were listening. That pleased the innkeeper little. He shouted through the laughter and music for her to stop. The dark soldier hurled some sharp invective at him and bade him offer the minstrel at least some wine and dinner for her skill.

"I can't afford to feed every wayfaring musician that wanders through here," the keeper shot back.

"You will if I've a mind."

The keeper commented on the soldier's parentage. A dirk bloomed in the post above the keeper's head.

"I said I've a mind to hear her play. And I will. Bring her wine and she can sit to table with us."

Eltheniel crowed her good fortune, silent as she was, and bowed to the soldier when he returned. Until supper was laid before her she played an assortment of tunes, all of human origin, and her patrons seemed well-pleased with her efforts. They had finished eating when she began. Their scrutiny disturbed her. What if they should discover who she was? The dark hair and tinted skin seemed enough to hide her identity, but she hadn't thought about manners and accent. Up until now she'd had to speak little, display few gestures which could confirm her as human.

Hunger worked for her. She broke the bread roughly, plunging it into the aromatic plate of stew and stuffed the dripping chunk into her mouth. Sauce dripped down her chin. She towelled it away with a sleeve. She didn't even consider utensils when she plucked morsels into her fingers.

"A little hungry are you?" the dark soldier commented.

She shrugged, answering around a mouthful, "Musicians eat when they may."

"Down from the north?"

"Aye." She passed the other a glance, marking his predatory face. "Heard minstrels were wanting at His Lordship's. Thought I might be a bit of different."

173

"That you are," the other commented.

She deflected that, pushed away the polished plate and again took up her flute. A series of ballads and lullabies followed, and they with a jig, more wine and laughter so that by the time she slid her instrument inside her sleeve the soldiers were free enough in their comments that she might try a few questions.

"Is that where you're headed – to the castle?"

The dark one shook his head, tipping his cup. "The opposite direction."

"Pity."

He raised a brow.

"I would have welcomed some company on my journey there. Travelling alone – it tends to weary a person."

The other said, "You'll not have any problem finding company. Not with craft like yours. Wouldn't surprise me but Raxis takes a liking to your tunes, Minstrel. There's something sweet in the way you play."

He was heading too near the mark for her liking. As hard as she'd tried to stay away from the elven way of music, it seemed she hadn't tried hard enough. "You think I'll stand a good chance of winning a place in court?"

"Better than most. He's in a foul temper these days."

"Things not going well? I'd heard some talk up north but paid it no heed."

"You might. There's an elf on the loose he wants back and until we find her there'll be no peace in or out of the castle."

"Another tune," the dark one said, his eyes glittering, "to pay for your supper."

The flute had just touched her lip when he tossed his cup into her face. He grinned. She lurched to her feet, heart fluttering against her ribs. The bench crashed to the floor behind her, upsetting a log from the fire which rolled out a sheaf of flame onto the wood. He lunged across the table for her. Someone shouted. Another joined in. She couldn't see the door for the wine in her eyes. Blindly, she leapt away from the table, fell over someone, felt arms close around hers, screamed, wrenched away and drove to the door. Coldness hit her hard. She flew down the stairs despite the darkness. Men cursed behind her.

When she hit the ground she wiped her sleeve across her eyes, still ran, hoping she would out-distance them just a little. Her fingers groped for the silver at her breast. The moon had just started to rise over the hills before her. Her spell wouldn't be strong. There was no time for preparation. Silver light burst over her. She turned and hurled a word toward the tavern, spun and fled. Confusion would tangle them for just a little while.

And the Angels Sang

Still she ran, out of the village, down the road to where it branched. Fear of capture was greater than her fear of the bog and she waded hip deep into the black mire. Rushes stood like spears across her path. She felt her hair floating around her on the water. She slowed, afraid of losing her footing. Every sense in her screamed to run, but she kept an even pace, pushing through the scum that now reached mid-chest.

At last she began to rise. Any warmth she'd had was now spent, her teeth chattering, her limbs trembling. Step after step brought her out of the swamp, to the road, and the enormous hill before her. It was only instinct that pushed her into a run and then it seemed as if a lifetime had been squandered before she crested the hill, gulping mouthfuls of air as she stood, staring.

Years of disuse and Raxis' men had taken the fineness from the ring of stones that circled the plateau depression, but even that didn't mar Fionelthen's beauty. Lit by the rising moon it was silver, ring within ring of stone and stone girdled by enormous trees that had once been their homes, now blackened from fire and reaching like claws to the spangled sky. Into the centre plunged a path she had walked many times. It led to the heart of everything elven.

She sank to her knees, weary, heartsick, and wept.

A curse rose up the hill to her. Eltheniel jumped to her feet and ran. She must reach and stay at the centre of the rings until the moon passed directly overhead, as it would tonight. Whatever happened after that didn't matter.

From this height Fionelthen was deceivingly small. This she knew. It was a trick of the land, the way it bent and made distances seem trivial. That would be an advantage to her once the soldiers came over the hill; she would know her way. They would not.

She flew toward the central ring. Tears all but blinded her. There would be no hope after she was done, yet little was left if she didn't finish the spell she had begun when Fionelthen had been put under siege. Years she endured Raxis' roughness, all to set the second cant of the spell. It would be finished tonight.

When she stood panting in a ring of white stone that was the centre, several arrows had fallen short of their mark. For now she crouched behind the altar stone, wishing the moon to rise. It must be near its mark because the runes ringing the floor were pale, little shadow.

Leather scraped stone. A whisper hissed around her. She held her breath, her fingers clutching the silver flash.

"Where are you, Elf?" one of them said.

A Memory of Moonlight and Silver

She chanced a look at the open sky above her. The moon, round, white, had only a little to travel before it filled the centre ring. Despite herself she couldn't stop trembling.

"What things did you sacrifice on this altar?"

Fools, she thought. They only had mind for brutality. How could she explain that a dying elf offered themselves upon the altar. It was a bier. Moonlight and magic did the rest. This place was holy. There would be no blood spilled within this ring of stone, else its magic would die. She was too close to her mark to let it die yet.

They were close now. She passed a glance to the moon. Hurry! Hurry!

"It would be better for you if you came back. Raxis will spare the rest of the elves if you give yourself up. It's you he wants."

She remembered the friends who had fallen because of her stubbornness and Raxis' ruthlessness. Every week another had died when she refused to yield the lore of the elves to him. It had not been without cost to her. She had felt herself falling deeper and deeper into hopelessness. Almost she had given in. What was she against his kind of world? It was something she realized bitterly. A passing of ages was in hand. Yet she wouldn't give him something as dangerous as what she knew. That would be folly.

The light in the ring was bright now, intolerably white, blinding. Both soldiers swore. Cautiously, she peered over the edge of the altar only to find them shielding their eyes from the brilliance of the moon which was directly overhead. There would be little time.

She rose, yanked the chain from her bodice and held the flash in her fingers, tilted to the moon. Argence bounded from the flash to the sky. Threads of light fell to the runes, increasing in brilliance till the soldiers were no more than shadows. They groaned, crossing themselves.

Now Eltheniel chanted. The words were not sweet, "*Angrethen thangst est,*" and her face wet with tears. She did nothing to hide them.

The soldiers were on their knees. Still her chant grew, as the light grew and now reached out to the next ring of stones. She ripped the thong from her neck and set the flash upon the altar, bolting for the path. Power prickled along her back as she fled. Behind her the light swelled, as if the moon were merging with the earth, spilling from one ring to another, and still she ran, exhausted but ran, desperate to reach the outer ring before the light. She did and there repeated the chant one last time.

Her flight took her far up into the hills where humans were reluctant to go. She threw herself down just as the first explosions shook the earth. Another rumbled in the distance. She whirled. There was a pinpoint of whiteness on the distant ridge of mountains, the mountains where Raxis had built his castle. Below her burned a ball of silver flames. She thought of the elves who had died tonight away from their elven home, and also of the humans who had been innocent of Raxis' crimes. There had been no other way to keep elven power out of his hands.

Had she killed herself, and Raxis lived, he would have plied countless elves for what little they knew and in the end had the sum of what Eltheniel knew.

As things stood, she was now the last elf, with no one to know of her exile and so she watched the twin explosions until dawn when they faded, as the time of the elves would fade like a memory of moonlight and silver.

Afterword

In the genesis of any work there is always that spark of inspiration that sends my imagination in a new orbit. That spark could be anything: an article, a concept, a person.

The cover story, And the Angels Sang, sprang from the historical accounts of the torture of Father Jean de Brebeuf. The Norman Brebeuf (1593 to 1649) was a Jesuit missionary who braved the perils of Canada's wilderness, several times making the arduous 800 mile journey from Trois Rivieres to Georgian Bay where he eventually established the mission, Ste. Marie among the Hurons which has been reconstructed on the original site at Midland, Ontario. His grave is still there, a powerful presence.

A peaceable man, intelligent, an adept diplomat, Brebeuf compiled one of the first Huron/French dictionaries, left extensive notes on the customs and diplomatic procedures of the Hurons, and it is alleged didn't cry out during the long hours of his torture at the hands of the Iroquois.

As an adjunct to Brebeuf's story, I read accounts of trauma victims experiencing out-of-body sensations, and that surreal quality, combined with what was clearly Brebeuf's own devotion to not only his God, but the people he came to serve, formed the foundation of the story.

While I was writing And the Angels Sang, I was also writing the novel Shadow Song, which deals very much with Ojibwa culture. In my research of these two stories, I came across an Inuit legend, Sister Sun. Like many of the Arctic native people's myths, this one is embedded in violence and darkness, perhaps a reflection of the environment they endure.

The legend, along with a fascination of the foundation for legend, gave rise to my story, Sister Sun. The story appears as it did when published in On Spec, employing past tense for present occurrences, against present tense for past. I chose this literary device as a way of conveying the immediacy of the creation of legend, that Yukio's past has caused his future, and is, as a result, of greater importance than his present.

Have a Nice Day and Pass the Arsenic was one of my early publication successes, and written as an illustration that basic human needs will always remain no matter where we go or what we do.

Protector, on the other hand, arose out of the loneliness of a listener and Jungian-based Myers-Briggs personality profiling, specifically an INFJ, (also known as Counsellor/Idealist) which is the profile I seem to fit. Apparently (depending on the source) about two percent of the world's population are

INFJ. This personality profiling was set against what I perceive to be an increasingly irresponsible and uncaring Western society.

While exploring the dynamics of human relationships the whole concept of reality rattled in my brain, and that lead to a brief dip into the world of string-theory (that made my brain hurt, sort of a stop-that it's-wonderful!) Out of that investigation arose *The Gift*, and what is now an outline for a novel, *Caliban*. Despite the fact some people see the tale as a ghost story, it was never my intention. For me *The Gift* explores a man's perceived descent into madness, set against a character so alien she is capable of altering reality

Over-Exposed is purely about relationships, and the depths of love, a concept made all the more poignant recently by the heart-breaking life of Robert Latimer to whom I can only send all my very best thoughts. My story also examines the view of an artist and how that artist sees his world.

I swung back to string-theory (the concept that there are up to twelve space/time dimensions, all coexisting) in the story, *Zero Mile*, which was my way of examining human obsession with being bigger, better, faster. Watching Olympic athletes compete, I can only wonder just how much can be shaved from records before finally it is acceptable and the norm to allow body enhancements? And then, at what cost to humanity?

Darkies returns to the dynamics, and sometimes devastations, of human relationships, as does *A Case of Time*, although the latter also grew out of an interest in what is learned behaviour and instinctive, and the question: can either be erased once part of our neuro-chemical makeup.

Jaguar was one of the stories slated for workshop at Clarion 1989, before I stood on my idealistic principles, packed my bags, and left after three weeks. The story arose out what was to prove a prophetic belief that fresh water would become a traded commodity, one valuable enough to attract criminal profit-seekers.

The last story of this somewhat dark, speculative section, *The Green Season*, was also written while I attended Clarion, and found its creation after study of the social behaviour of lions, although I admit to the cardinal sin of anthropomorphism.

The latter section, *Sariel*, being fantasy is lighter in nature and definitely reflects my inner child, and it is out of that sense of wonder, and a love of the great age of sail, that the story *For a Cup of Tea* gave birth. Originally written specifically for a British anthology a colleague from Clarion was editing. The story is a fantastical alternative history to the famed race between *Cutty Sark* and *Thermopylae* in 1872, which *Cutty Sark* lost by only one week despite loosing her rudder in a storm and carrying on with an improvisation.

Unfortunately the story received my editor's ire; I was accused of chauvinism and blatant sexual references denigrating to women. That reaction always puzzled me. Plainly *On Spec* didn't find the story offensive and purchased it.

Summer Wine and Sweet Mistresses, one of my early short stories, and first sale, blatantly reflects my love of trees and the dryad myth.

Like *For a Cup of Tea*, *Dragonslayer* was written for a specific market and failed for the same reason. The anthology for which the story was targeted was an examination of what happened to all the fantasy heroes after the wars were over. I'm afraid I didn't approach the subject with sufficient seriousness. All I could envision was some swaggering archetype reduced to selling life insurance (no offence to insurance salespeople). It just seemed the ultimate irony.

The third time I wrote a short story for a specific market, Marion Zimmer Bradley's *Sword & Sorceress* X, I hit my mark. I thought it would be interesting to examine a tale from a deity's point of view. Clearly the very helpful and remarkable MZB thought the same.

In *A Dishwasher for Michelina* I thought it would be fun to visit what would happen to an ordinary fellow, with an ordinary life, who was suddenly blessed with a legendary money tree. It was meant as nothing more than a whimsical romp.

While darker in nature, *A Memory of Moonlight and Silver* is also part of my whimsy, little say my love of elves and the loss of them in our lives.

As a sidebar to that, when first we moved to this old stone house, I dreamed one of my remarkable, very real dreams, wherein on the crown of the hill of our property, beneath the apple tree and adjacent an old well, convened the royal court of the Sidhe of Neustadt. They decreed Gary and I would be allowed to share this land with them so long as our son, Adam, would act as liaison and ambassador. I must check with Adam on his progress there.